The Lost War

Karl K. Gallagher

Published by Kelt Haven Press, Saginaw, TX.

Cover art by eBookLaunch.com.
Editing by Laura Gallagher.
Audio Recording by Laura Gallagher.

Arrival

"If you don't pick a name, you'll wind up as Newman Greenhorn," said his girlfriend.

"I like that," said Newman.

"Fine," she said. "From now on you're Newman and I'm Goldenrod."

If going by a funny name was the price of seeing his girlfriend in that outfit he'd pay it. The rigid front of her blue dress pressed her breasts up into a mesmerizing display of cleavage. Her pale gold hair was coiled in a green net behind her head. The forest green cords were just a shade darker than her eyes.

He glanced around the dirt parking lot to make sure no car was coming down their lane then looked back at Goldenrod's beautiful face. When Newman first met her he'd teasingly compared her to a Barbie doll. Now it was his turn to be a Ken doll. Her eyes surveyed him top to bottom.

He didn't know what she could find wrong with his outfit. It was a green shirt stretching down to his knees and loose tan pants. The shoes were a finer version of the leather moccasins he'd made as a boy scout.

Goldenrod reached up to tug Newman's black cloth cap to one side. "There. It should cover your left ear."

Next she fiddled with his brown leather belt, tightening the knot that replaced a buckle. He fought down the temptation to suggest more fiddling. A busy parking lot in daylight was no place for that. He was 29 now, a few years older than her, and couldn't act like a teenager.

"You're all set now, my lord Newman. Let's go to the war!" She grabbed the handle of her three foot long cart, loaded with enough clothes and food for the weekend. Newman lifted his dufflebag out of the trunk of her car and slammed the lid. He hefted his wooden bow and arrows in his other hand as he followed her across the parking lot.

Newman studied the cars for clues about what these people would be like. Most had some wear. None were shiny and new. They wouldn't throw away something that worked. Half the cars bore a sticker with the stylized castle of "The Kingdom", the medieval historical reenactors Goldenrod spent a third of her weekends with.

Calling the event a "war" hadn't encouraged him to come. To Goldenrod the word meant playing dress-up with friends. To him "war" was being a long way from home, eating terrible food, and strangers trying to kill him. They were going to spend the weekend playing at swordfighting and crafting and hopefully doing some partying. Not his idea of a "war."

Two women sat behind a picnic table at the edge of the parking lot beside a path going into a narrow line of trees. One wore a plain dress of brown wool. Her hair hung down to her waist in a tight braid. Two enameled medallions hung around her neck.

The other woman had to be portraying nobility. A black velvet jacket adorned with pearls partially covered a shimmering silk dress. A complicated hat with multiple feathers sat on her head.

"Lady Foxglove, Lady Verbena, this is Newman. It's his first event," explained Goldenrod. He had to sign a couple of forms before following Goldenrod down the path.

Ten yards later the trees stopped, and The Kingdom began. When Goldenrod said "tents," he'd imagined the olive drab Army tents he was deployed in, or the flimsy pop-ups he'd slept in as a Boy Scout.

Here white canvas was formed into shelters of all shapes and sizes. Rectangles, ovals, cones, pyramids. Decorations ranged from strips of color along a roofline to roofs painted with coats of arms. A wedge that would be cramped for two people sat next to a massive structure the Army would use for a mess hall.

Newman realized the tents all faced in, toward a small opening between the mess hall and an ornate tent Goldenrod called "the royal pavilion." Lanes between tents went out from there, and the tents were in circles around it. A few nylon pop-up tents designed for whole families sat to the outside as if ashamed of their modernity.

The people were even more varied than the tents. Ages ranged from an old woman with a bamboo walker to a toddler in a red shirt and no pants trying to escape his big sister. Like the ladies at the entrance, clothes could be as simple as a plain tunic to layered and embroidered suits out of a royal portrait. Skin color mostly matched the tent canvas, with a handful of darker people. Many wore decorated metal crowns on their heads, receiving deferential nods from passers-by.

Goldenrod said, "House Applesmile won't be here until sunset. We'll have to find a place to leave the cart until then."

"Lady Goldenrod!" The speaker was tall and muscular, about Newman's own age. His wide smile split a tan face. He wore a thick cloth shirt with leather ties dangling from the shoulders and elbows.

"Hi, Strongarm. Good to see you. This is my boyfriend, Newman Greenhorn."

"Pleased to meet you, Newman," he said with extroverted friendliness and possibly a trace of disappointment. The stranger made his handshake a test of strength. Newman had played that game before. They ended equally sore.

"Are you camping alone?" asked Goldenrod.

"I'm with the Wolfheads." He pointed at a foursome of red-roofed tents.

"Can we leave our cart there? I want to give him the full tour."

"We can ask."

Mistress Vixen declared they had plenty of room, and were welcome to spend the night if House Applesmile was delayed.

"Good," said Goldenrod. "Time for tour. No, wait, I should see Mistress Seamchecker about the inkles first."

Strongarm volunteered to take Newman under his wing while Goldenrod handled her "art stuff." Newman quickly found himself watching armored knights practicing swordsmanship. The swords were wood, but the armor was all steel and leather.

"Going to make Goldenrod Queen?" asked Strongarm.

"She told me about the crown tournaments, but I don't know if she even wants to be queen," answered Newman. Making the winner of a sword fight and his consort absolute rulers for six months struck him as silly, but it seemed to work for these people.

Strongarm laughed. "Every woman in the Kingdom wants to be queen. Come on, give it a try."

He asked Count Dirk's permission to bring in a trainee. The Count looked Newman over for a moment. He was a wiry older man, at least forty, with a bit of grey in his short black hair. Then he offered his back-up armor as a loan. Fifteen minutes later Newman walked onto the field—no, the "eric"—in full medieval fighting panoply.

Strongarm waited in his armor, holding a shield painted with an arm flexing its bicep.

Count Dirk looked them over. "Lay on!" He stayed outside the ropes marking the square.

Strongarm hopped toward Newman, sword pointed back over his shoulder, shield under his chin.

Newman stood still, sword in front of him, held straight up.

Strongarm circled to his shield-side. Newman moved to keep the center of the eric between them.

"Good footwork," said Count Dirk.

Newman lifted his shield to block an overhand blow at his head. His return swing tapped Strongarm's shield.

Count Dirk caught Strongarm's eye. He tapped the back of his head.

Strongarm nodded, then closed up tight to Newman. He fended off a sword blow with his shield, then used it to press Newman's shield against his body, rendering it useless.

A step with his right foot let him reach past Newman's head. He flipped his wrist to bring the sword around. Leaning back added the weight of his body as the yard of rattan wood smacked into the rear of Newman's helmet.

Newman's foot hooked the back of Strongarm's knee, pulling him off-balance. As he tilted, Newman's armored elbow struck the other's helm with a clang that stopped the fighting on the other three erics. Strongarm landed on his side and lay still.

Newman took two steps back, pivoting left and right to look for other enemies. "Shit, that was a foul, wasn't it? Sorry."

"Hold!" shouted Count Dirk. "Hold, hold!" He ducked under the rope and advanced on Newman. "Ground your sword and shield."

"I'm fine," said Strongarm. "I'm fine. Just surprised me, is all." He didn't try to get up.

Dirk ignored him, solely focused on Newman, who'd obediently dropped his weapon. "Helm off."

Newman tried, but needed the count's help with the straps. When it came off, his face looked pale and sweatier than the exercise justified. He breathed rapidly and glanced side to side.

"We need to talk, son." Count Dirk led Newman to some oaks beyond the edge of the camp. A pair of squires enjoying the shade scampered away at his wave.

"Now. We get some martial artists in occasionally. Putting thirty pounds of steel on them usually makes them start from scratch."

"I'm used to this much weight, sir."

"Uh-huh. Military training?"

"Yes, sir. And . . . some experience."

"Want to talk about it?"

"No."

"You don't have to." Pause. "Unless you ever want try fighting again, heavy or rapier. Then you'll explain your background and issues to me or whoever's in charge first. Clear?"

"Yes, my lord."

"I'm a Count. You call me Your Excellency."

"Yes, your excellency."

"Right. Go apologize to Strongarm then we'll get you out of the gear."

Strongarm refused the apology, claiming it was all his fault for not asking any questions beforehand. He promised Newman a beer as compensation.

They found Goldenrod before turning up any brew. "Having fun?" she asked.

"Yes," said Newman.

Goldenrod continued the tour. Scribes working on illuminated scrolls received polite praise from Newman. The blacksmith shop caught his attention. The smith hadn't warmed the forge. He was using an anvil to support a steel helmet as he hammered a dent out of it.

"Evenin'" grunted the smith.

Goldenrod introduced them. "Master Forge, this is Newman Greenhorn."

"Welcome. Are you interested in smithing?"

"I've done some metal repair. Is this a portable workshop?"

The smith grinned. "Aye, it's a single trailer. The forge and both anvils are on a frame. When I get it to a flat spot I crank up the axle until the wheels are off the ground. Abracadabra—a solid workshop."

"How do the tires handle the heat?"

"Oh, the wheels are unbolted before I fire up the forge. But that's apprentice work." He gave Newman a speculative glance. "One of my apprentices couldn't make it this weekend. Want to learn the art?"

"I'll think on it, my lord. I have to find out the schedule for the archery tournament first."

"Not a worry. Come by any time, we can find some work for you."

Newman turned back to Goldenrod. She was chatting with a tall redhead her own age.

"Newman, this is my friend Redinkle. We're staying with her family."

He flushed as Redinkle scanned him from head to toe.

"So that's the guy, huh? Not too shabby. Good to meet you, Newman."

"Good to meet you, my lady."

"Oh, I'm no lady. Goldenrod's the one impressing all the artists and nobles. C'mon, Dad should have the trailer at our spot by now."

Redinkle's 'should' hadn't counted on the narrow gap between the trees and neighboring tents. Her father was unhooking the open-topped trailer from his SUV about sixty feet from the empty campsite.

"Let's get to pushing, boys," he said, as his wife drove the SUV away. Two younger men joined him at the back of the trailer and leaned into it. Newman grabbed the front corner and pulled.

Redinkle walked ahead, calling left and right to steer them clear of trees and tents. They avoided collisions until just before their campsite. A wheel brushed against a tent stake, knocking it out of the ground.

Fortunately, the neighbor tent was held up by enough ropes that losing one didn't endanger it. When the trailer stopped Newman walked back to the tent, stretched its rope out taut and shoved the stake through the loop at the end a couple inches into the dirt.

One of the trailer pushers said, "Gimme a minute and I'll get the sledge out."

Newman stomped on the stake, driving it almost another foot into the ground.

The stranger blinked. "It usually takes a few taps with a three pound sledge to get one of those in."

"I weigh more than three pounds."

"Guess so. I'm Pernach. Thanks for helping us out. You're Goldenrod's guy?"

"That's me," Newman said. 'Goldenrod's Guy' felt like a more solid identifier than 'Newman Greenhorn.'

Pernach was married to Redinkle. She handled the rest of the introductions. "My parents, and the heads of House Applesmile, Master Sweetbread and Mistress Tightseam. My cousin Pinecone and his girlfriend Shellbutton."

"Unloading time," said Sweetbread.

Newman tried to carry as much as he could. He kept being redirected to put things in a different pile. These people had developed an elaborate system for where to put everything for an efficient set-up. Baskets and chests to the outside, canvas in different places according to weight, and wooden poles where they'd be in the final position.

Tightseam and Shellbutton held flashlights to help them see in the gloom. The sun had set while they'd been wrangling the trailer.

The last poles—beams, really—were the heaviest. Newman was directed to put his in the center of the campsite. Sweetbread joined it with the other oversized pieces in a pi shape.

"Now the roof."

Newman and the other two young men carried the heaviest pile of canvas into the middle. It unfolded into a rectangle.

"Corners up!"

The group split into pairs. Goldenrod handled inserting the spike of one pole through the metal grommet in the corner of the roof. Two ropes with loops on their ends went onto the spike.

"Now lift it straight up," she said.

The pole wasn't much weight for Newman, even if it was a foot taller than him. Pulling the heavy canvas off the ground made it an effort.

"Good!" called Sweetbread. "Move them out some, we want the sides straight."

Newman had to shift a couple of feet to take up slack. When Sweetbread was happy with everyone's position Goldenrod put a pair of heavy tent stakes in the ground and looped the ropes loosely around them.

The roof would rise a few more feet above its end when finished. Right now it hung down blocking Newman's view of the other corners. He could hear the ring of a sledgehammer driving in metal stakes.

Sweetbread came to their corner last. "Neat job. You'd think you'd put up a tent before."

"I have, sir. Just not this kind."

"Fair enough." He drove in the last stake. "Let's get the ridgepole."

Newman and Pernach lifted the two supporting poles to hold the ridgebeam against the center of the roof. Sweetbread and Pinecone slid the blunt spikes on the poles into grommets, then tied fabric strips hanging from the roof around the beam.

"Doesn't the roof stay on by its weight?" asked Newman.

"Depends on how much wind we get," said Sweetbread. "I've seen storms pull a tent right off its poles. That's the last. Lift, now. Slowly. Keep them at the same angle."

Newman matched his pole to Pernach's. In moments they were vertical. It felt like a tent now, a very big and roomy one.

"Side poles now," said Sweetbread.

A dozen more poles were spread among the four sides. Then all the gear was brought inside before they hung the canvas walls from the roof.

"Free time," announced the master of the house when the walls were done.

"Oh, good," said Goldenrod. "Let's go get our gear."

***

Goldenrod had packed sandwiches for Friday night so they wouldn't have to cook. She led him into the mess hall, which she called the 'common pavilion,' a huge tent filled with tables. Most were packed with people in a variety of costumes—no, *garb*. A woman waved from the end of a table. Goldenrod hugged her before sitting down. "Lady Buttercup, I'm pleased to present my friend Newman Greenhorn."

Buttercup shook hands firmly. "Welcome, Newman. First event?"

"Yes'm. I mean, yes, my lady." He realized she was at the end of the table because her wheelchair was blocked by the built-in benches.

"Oh, don't be fancy with me, I'm an artist, not a duchess."

"Newman's an archer," Goldenrod supplied.

"Going to compete in the tourney?"

Newman nodded. "It's been a few years since I've done any shooting, so I don't expect to do well, but it'll be fun to use my bow again."

"Is it a compound?" Buttercup asked. Modern bows were banned from the competition.

"I have a couple of those but didn't bring them. I'm using a composite I made myself for a merit badge project."

Buttercup's brows lifted. She turned back to Goldenrod. "Your young man has some talent for carpentry. But don't let them name him after the glue."

Goldenrod laughed.

"Wait," said Newman, "I don't get to pick a name?"

"You can try," said Buttercup. "If you pick something that fits and there's no one else using it you can make it stick. If you stay Newman too long we'll find something that fits you."

"Huh. I'd hate to get stuck with a name I hate."

"Well, you can change it. But that usually takes doing something spectacular or the King deciding to rename you."

"The King? Why would he care about someone's name?"

Buttercup chuckled. "That doesn't happen often. Last one was when King Stonefist decided Lady Chamomile should be Lady Burnout."

"What? Why'd he do that?" demanded Newman.

"Oh, she's an emergency room doc in mundane life, then she comes here and patches bruises for fun. Stonefist thought she needed to take some time off so he tagged her to shame her into taking some time for herself. Didn't work. She's working the chiurgeon tent this weekend."

***

Newman looked left and right to make sure he was properly spaced between Goldenrod and the stranger to his right. It didn't seem to matter. The couple dozen people forming the circle were sloppily arranged. Squeezing them between a couple of tents made it more of an oval than a circle. But he wanted to do his part right, even if he didn't know what he was supposed to be doing.

He'd said yes to Goldenrod's invitation to attend a pagan circle without thinking. Now he wished he'd asked some questions. This other religion didn't do anything the way he was used to. Everyone faced in toward the cluttered table in the center as the priestess called chants in different directions. He held up his eating knife, turned when the others did, and repeated "So mote it be" when everyone else did. Hopefully it wouldn't get any more complicated.

Priestess Belladonna did put on a good show. Her prayers were passionate, her calls to the gods detailed enough to educate him, and the ritual of blade and chalice made the sexual symbolism clear without any adolescent smirking. Now she seemed to start a sermon. "We all came here to seek something—a glimpse of a better past, association with our true peers, a chance to display our strengths, and usually some of all three." Belladonna turned, looking at each member of the circle in turn. "But we're also all fleeing something. We're seeking the same things and fleeing different things. Working together we can help each other escape."

Belladonna turned about and walked up to a woman in the circle. "What are you fleeing?"

"My ex," she answered.

"Cut yourself free," said Belladonna. She aimed her index finger at the ground at the woman's heels. To the next person in the circle she asked, "What are you fleeing?"

"My job."

"Cut yourself free." She put her hand on his wrist and angled his blade toward the grass. "Cut the ground and connect it to your neighbors' cuts, so all in the circle may be free." She went to the next. "What are you fleeing?"

"Poverty."

"Cut yourself free." The first two were kneeling to cut through the roots. The third joined them. Belladonna moved on, repeating her question and direction to each. The answers floated across the circle, some firm, some hesitant.

"My mother."

"Stalkers."

"Drugs."

"Family."

"Booze."

"Dad."

When Newman's turn came he was cheerful. Seeing others fumbling with how to do their part of the ritual made him feel an equal. It made sense to him. Cutting around the circle would symbolically cut all their ties to what they were trying to leave behind.

"What are you fleeing?" asked Belladonna.

"Guilt," answered Newman.

The priestess inclined her head gravely. "Cut yourself free."

Newman knelt to make his cut. Beside him Goldenrod said, "Boredom," and joined him.

They were among the last to answer Belladonna. After completing the circle, she moved to the center to urge everyone to finish. "Make your cuts complete! Your cut must join your neighbor's cut! The circle must be unbroken!"

Newman noticed Goldenrod's cut overlapped but didn't touch his. A swipe of his knife connected them. With their attention on the ground no one in the circle noticed the stars shift into new constellations.

Belladonna's black dress streamed out in a breeze between the tents. One of the corner candles nearly went out. "Ground your blades and hold hands," she ordered. "Feel your freedom. Share your energy with each other. You are released from what pursues you!" As she raised her hands to the sky the circle followed, clasped hands reaching up. "Let us thank the gods for their gifts."

The corner callers said thanks to their deities in turn. With the ceremony over the circle broke up, some clumping, others scattering.

"So?" said Goldenrod.

"It was . . . more powerful than I imagined," said Newman. "I feel free, energized, powerful."

"So do I," she said. "It's not usually this good. Belladonna has her, well, never mind, but she can run a circle."

"What's next?"

"Traditional midnight Steak & Shake run."

"Can I come?"

"Sure," she smiled. An older couple volunteered to join the expedition. Goldenrod introduced them as Beargut and Elderberry. Newman led them to the parking lot.

Rounding the last tent he stopped abruptly. A wall of trees was blocking the way. "Uh . . ."

"Wrong way?" asked Goldenrod.

"No, look. The path is clear, then it's just leaves."

"This isn't right," said Beargut. "I've been coming here for ten years. The trees aren't this dense, there's grass between them."

"Did we get turned around?" Newman asked. He looked left and right. The trees ended neatly a few yards from the tents. Too neatly. Some branches ended as if they'd been sliced with a bandsaw. He pointed them out.

"Do people trim trees to make room for their tents?"

"Never," said Elderberry. "It's prohibited by park rules. If we cut a tree we'd be banned from the site."

"I could have sworn this was the way to the parking lots," said Goldenrod.

"It is," agreed Beargut. "Should be right through there. But I don't see the streetlights."

Newman turned slowly on his heel. "There's no streetlights in any direction. I thought I saw some before the circle. Did the power go out?"

Goldenrod fished out her cell phone. "That might be it. I'm not getting any signal."

With tents hiding the few campfires around, the greatest source of light was above them. Newman looked up. "Wasn't the Moon gibbous? Now it looks half full."

"No, it's a crescent," said Elderberry. Their eyes followed each other's pointing arms. The foursome looked silently between the two moons. There really weren't any curse words strong enough.

"What the hell?" snapped Beargut. "Seriously, what the hell is going on?"

"We're someplace else. Not where we should be." Newman's face was a professional mask of calm, not something Goldenrod had seen on him before.

Elderberry whimpered and sat down. Beargut knelt next to her and wrapped his arms around her.

"If we moved . . ." Goldenrod paused for thought. "What moved us?"

Newman didn't answer. He turned his head back and forth, checking for threats in the unknown woods.

"Belladonna. I'd wondered why she'd asked the gods' protection on the whole camp. Usually we just call them to the circle. That bitch!" Goldenrod sprinted back to the circle. Newman followed, impressed with her ability to run in ankle-length skirts. His tunic kept getting caught between his knees and tripping him.

Belladonna was alone, packing candles and tables into a wheeled box.

"What did you do?" demanded Goldenrod.

"What we all asked for, my dear," said the priestess.

"I wanted more! I didn't want to give up everything, everyone I already had!"

"Maybe you should have phrased yourself more carefully."

"Bullshit. Something like this doesn't happen because of vague words. You set it up. Take us back."

Belladonna smirked. "The gods' gifts are not to be spurned."

"It's your will I'm spurning. Undo what you did!"

Belladonna laughed.

Goldenrod knocked her flat.

Newman was impressed. He hadn't thought she could pack that much of a wallop.

"Punish me all you wish," said the prone priestess. "It's done. Welcome to your new home."

Goldenrod kicked her in the stomach.

"You're spending the rest of your life here." Belladonna laughed.

As Goldenrod drew back for another kick Newman grabbed her shoulder. "Wait! We need to find out how she did it. With all of us working together maybe we can find a way to get home."

Belladonna rolled to her feet and started running. "You can't. I didn't do it alone," she said over her shoulder. Goldenrod gave chase, Newman close behind.

The priestess followed the shortest path through the tents to the woods. As she disappeared between the trunks Newman grabbed Goldenrod's arm. "We can't follow her in there."

"She's getting away!"

"We don't know what's in these woods. There could be something dangerous. It's night."

Goldenrod pulled her arm free but stood still. "I hope the worst thing ever happens to you!" she yelled into the woods.

***

Constable liked patrolling in the wee hours. It was quiet, the parties were smaller, and people were calmer. A dwindling party would invite him to help finish off a bottle. An achy matron was willing to gossip. Some other insomniacs weren't feeling chatty. They traded polite nods with him.

He kept his path inside the outer ring of tents. People heading off to the bushes didn't want anyone spotting them. It wasn't his job to keep them out of trouble. He just watched for people in trouble in camp.

That girl in the black dress looked to be in some trouble. Constable watched her long enough to be sure the limp wasn't from tripping over a tent stake. She was hunched over and clutching herself. "My lady, are you all right?"

"Yes, I'm, I'm fine." She didn't look up. Her dress was filthy, dirt and pine needles all over the back.

"May I escort you to your tent?"

She recognized his tabard. "Yes, thank you, Constable."

"Where are you staying?"

"With the Green Stag."

"Lean on me, lass." He guided her around the tents. When they reached his destination he lifted the tent flap and followed her in. "Lady Burnout! Sorry to wake you ma'am, but this one's for you."

Belladonna tried to step back, bouncing off Constable's broad belly. Lady Burnout switched on the battery-powered lantern by her cot. The light revealed the chiurgeon's tent, examining table in the middle. "What's the matter?"

"Nothing," said Belladonna.

Lady Burnout threw off her blanket. Her nightgown was thicker than Belladonna's dress. She stood and held up the lantern before the younger woman's face. "Split lip, bruises, black eye. Right. Have a seat on the table and we'll take a look at your nothing."

Constable excused himself, letting the flap fall closed.

"I just fell."

"Uh-huh. Well, let me see how bad the fall was so I know what pain meds to give you." Burnout studied Belladonna's walk as she stepped to the table and stiffly hoisted her hips onto the edge. The chiurgeon circled the table then stopped in front of her patient. "Where's it hurt the most?"

"All over. My legs, I guess."

"Okay." Lady Burnout hung the lantern from a hook and opened a box of swabs. "Did you get right up or lay there a bit?"

"Took a few minutes to catch my breath."

Burnout grabbed Belladonna's ankle and yanked straight up. The patient fell on her side with a screech. The cotton swab swiped between her legs. "You bitch! How dare you!"

Ziplocks were stored under the table. Burnout dropped the swab into one and squeezed the air out. "Poor woman's rape kit."

"I didn't consent to that!"

"No. But I've seen dozens like you come into the ER so I know tomorrow, after a nap and a meal and a shower, you'll decide you want to press charges after all. But it's too late to get a sample then. So you didn't consent, this can't be used as evidence, but when tomorrow you decide to consent the sample will be waiting."

"I wasn't raped."

"You're just being fucking insulting now." Burnout tapped her shoulder. "Loose dirt." Tap on the hip. "Dirt ground in to the fabric." She stepped back. "One hand-sized bruise on each wrist. Two-hand bruises on ankles. You were raped. There were at least four of them." She held the ziplock up to the lantern. "And one had some nasty VD. Orange is new on me. But all the rest I've seen plenty of times before."

"I don't have to tell you anything."

"No, you don't. Wish you'd think about the next girl who goes off by herself. I ought to call 911 anyway."

"Go ahead."

Slightly surprised, Burnout retrieved her cell phone from the pile by her cot. "Crap. No signal. I had four bars at dinner. I'll try again later."

"Can I go now?"

"Let's get some antiseptic on those injuries first. And I meant it about giving you some pain pills."

After treating the scrapes and giving Belladonna some water to wash the pills down with, Burnout checked her phone again. "Still no signal."

Her patient didn't offer any explanation of the lack of connection.

"Look, if we can't get 911 we can have someone drive you to the hospital."

Belladonna shook her head. "I just want to go back to my tent and lie down."

The chiurgeon sighed. "Will you make a report to Constable so we have a record of it?"

"I tripped and fell. Can I go now?"

Lady Burnout let her leave.

***

Newman woke as the stars began to fade. He dressed quietly to not bother anyone else in House Applesmile's tent. The household had stayed up late in a whispered debate over what could have relocated them until Master Sweetbread declared lights-out. The noise, or maybe the empty side of their sleeping bag, was enough to wake Goldenrod. She pulled on her dress and shoes without asking why. He slung his quiver over his shoulder and picked up his bow.

Once they stepped out of the tent Goldenrod asked, "What's that for?"

"Security blanket."

There was one oak tree between the tent and the strange new trees. He studied the bark and leaves. The trunks said 'elm' to him but the heart-shaped leaves didn't fit. He turned left at the edge of the forest and started walking.

"What are you looking for?" asked Goldenrod.

"I'm getting a feel for the terrain. Where are we, are there any threats out there, are there better places to be?" Newman kept his eyes outward, just glancing down enough to pick a clear path.

Goldenrod stayed to the inside of him. The camp was familiar. The woods . . . would have felt just fine to her if she'd expected them. That they'd appeared from nowhere was scary.

The scary trees thinned out on the west side of the camp. The dawn sun was at their back, so this was still west. Newman led her through a thin line of trees and stopped on the other side.

They stood on a river bluff, some sixty feet above the flood plain. The river was wide enough to sail on and too fast to swim in. Another bluff rose on the far side, crowned by forest.

Last night this spot had been a grass lawn sloping gently down to an artificial pond.

Goldenrod said, "You'd think after seeing two moons I'd expect things to be different."

"I think everything is going to keep surprising us," said Newman.

He looked up and down the river valley, examining every bend and knot for clues about this new place. A wrack of dead tree trunks and branches hung up in a bend caught his eye.

"There's no litter," he said.

"You sound like that's bad."

"No trash, or boards, or broken rafts means no people. We're alone here."

Goldenrod slid an arm around his waist. "We have each other. There's a lot of good people in the Kingdom. We'll manage."

He returned the embrace. "This is a good place for the camp. As close to the river as we can get and still be safe from floods."

"Maybe someone's looking out for us."

Behind them the camp was waking up. People who normally would have slept in were jolted from their beds by shouts of shock or simple surprise.

A herald called out, "Oyez! Their Majesties command all subjects to attend Court at this time! All subjects are commanded to attend!" He moved to a different part of the camp and repeated the call.

Newman and Goldenrod walked toward the center of the camp. People were arguing as they came in. There were shouts and screams as some who hadn't realized the change had it pointed out to them. A few were in hysterics. They were settled down gently or forcefully as needed. One man began punching at random until a blow from behind dazed him. Someone steered him along with the crowd into the open space before the royal pavilion.

The front wall of the pavilion was held up by poles to make an awning over several fancy chairs. Everyone stood. Some had folding chairs. A dozen fancy-clothed people came in. Four sat. The herald directed the crowd to sit. Those nearest to the pavilion plunked down on the grass. The folding chairs went behind them. Newman and Goldenrod were in the outer ring, standing with the rest.

"Who are these people?" asked Newman, looking at the ones sitting in the fancy chairs. The seats were portable thrones, carved with the Kingdom's heraldry and tall enough to provide a headrest.

Goldenrod pointed to the couple in the closest thrones. He was blonde, looked a bit over thirty, and wore a gold crown and an embroidered red velvet tunic tight enough to show off the muscles of his arms and shoulders. The woman next to him was slim, looking like the matching crown was too heavy for her. Her face was paler than his, lacking the sunburn. Thin hands twisted nervously in her lap. Her dress was gold, adorned with hundreds of beads. An older woman stood behind her. Goldenrod said, "King Estoc and Queen Camellia rule the Kingdom. They're halfway through their six month reign. The one in the gold dress behind them is Baroness Stitches, the chief lady-in-waiting. Sort of their organizer."

Next she indicated the couple in the second pair of thrones, set to the side and slightly behind Estoc and Camellia's. The man was black, dark enough to make Newman wonder if he was an African immigrant. His crown sat on top of a purple turban, which went with the Moorish style of his tunic. He was the calmest man in sight, his expression unperturbed by the disaster or the panicking people around them. His wife was nearly as serene, her ebony face turned up in a slight smile to mask her concern. Goldenrod continued, "King Ironhelm and Queen Dahlia are the Invaders. Or Visitors when we're being polite. This event is a war between our kingdom and theirs." Her voice caught. "Or it was before whatever-it-was happened."

Then she pointed to a man in a fur-trimmed black robe. He was older than the others, hair and beard streaked with grey. "That's Master Sharpquill, the Autocrat. He's in charge of the war—this camp."

"The King's not in charge?"

"Officially he is, but he just does the ceremonial stuff and blesses the consensus. The King reigns. The Autocrat rules. Well, rules this event. There'd be another Autocrat at the next event. Except. Well. We're not going home on Monday I guess."

After finishing opening formalities, the herald hushed the crowd for an address from King Estoc.

"Good morning, everyone." The king's smile made him look even more boyish. His voice had a slight catch. "We have a situation here. I'm sure it's scary for everyone. But there's lots of talented people here. Please stay calm and work together and I'm sure we'll all be fine. My lord Autocrat?"

The older man came forward as King Estoc returned to his throne.

"Not bad," whispered Goldenrod.

"Huh?"

"For someone who doesn't do anything but heavy fighting it's a decent speech."

Estoc had been trying to hide nervousness. Master Sharpquill looked as if landing in the wilderness was a routine annoyance for him. Possibly he was just too tired to care.

"In case anyone hasn't noticed yet, we're not where we set up camp. We're not on Earth, and our amateur astronomer assures me we're not in the Solar System, unless we're millions of years in the past or future."

Some moans came from those who'd hoped they could get home. Some who'd suppressed their panic in hopes of better news lost control. It took a couple minutes to calm the populace to where the Autocrat could speak again.

"How and why is a mystery. I'm going to request that you save discussing that mystery for after dark. We have lots of work to do. We can't afford to have two hundred people standing around arguing.

"Today only I want everyone to stay in camp. We're going to send out some scouts to check for danger. Today's task is inventory. Every household count your food and medicine. Assume you need to make your supplies last seven days. If you're short on food, or can spare some, see Countess Fennel.

"If you don't belong to a household . . ." the Autocrat ran through several more procedural issues. When he'd checked off everything on the index card in his hand he shoved it into a sleeve. "Now. It's clear this is an emergency. We need to pull together to survive it. As much fun as our usual debating of every question is there's no time for it right now. I ask you all: will you work as hard as you can to assure the survival of us all?"

A ragged chorus of "aye" came from the crowd.

"Will you accept temporary sacrifices for the good of us all?"

A firmer "aye" this time.

"Will you accept the emergency orders of the Crown to guide us all?"

"Aye!"

"On behalf of the Crown I thank you, and swear to do our best for you all. Go, do your inventory, make plans for tomorrow."

The herald dismissed the populace. A storm of chatter sprang up.

Newman whispered in Goldenrod's ear. "Wait, we're just leaving the same people in charge in an emergency?"

She shrugged. "Who else? We'd starve to death getting this bunch to agree to any other way to run things."

A stranger addressed Newman. "You any good with that bow?"

"Yes, I think so." He wasn't sure if this man merited a 'my lord' or not.

"I'm Bodkin. I'm organizing a hunting party for tomorrow. Want to join?"

"Sure."

"Where will I find you?"

"House Applesmile."

The hunter nodded and walked off in search of his next recruit.

***

House Applesmile's banner bore a boar's head, smiling widely, around an apple. Their host fried up some "mess" on a griddle over a fire. Goldenrod and Newman's sausage and bread had been diced before going into the common scramble. The smell was delightful. Everyone kept drifting to downwind to get more of it.

A well-dressed noblewoman approached the tent, followed by two men in armor. The host hailed her. "Good day, Lady Stitches. I believe you know my household. Let me introduce our guests, Lady Goldenrod and Newman Greenhorn. This is Her Majesty's Chief Lady in Waiting." The last was spoken to make it clear to Newman he was being honored by the introduction.

"Good day, Master Sweetbread." Stitches nodded to the guests. "Well met."

"How may I serve you today, my lady?"

"With a tour of your kitchen," said Stitches, face stiff. "Their Majesties have ordered me to collect the inventory of food supplies." She waved the clipboard in her hand as evidence.

"Of course," said Sweetbread. The "kitchen" tent had its sides extended on poles for extra shade. "We came with enough to feed ten for five days. There's only the six of us but we entertain, of course. That bag is Goldenrod's—how much did you bring, dear?"

"Eight sausages and four loaves, plus some bananas," she said. "Just enough to get us to Sunday morning."

Sweetbread's supplies were more varied, including vegetables and spices. Stitches made terse notes. The guards watched without interest until the last chest was opened.

"And the traditional booze and candy," said Sweetbread.

"Ah, yes," said Stitches. "We'll have to take that with us."

"What?" The householder was sure he'd misheard.

Stitches recited, "Their Majesties have ordered all alcohol and luxury foods brought to court for safe-keeping, to avoid drunkenness and dissention. Guards, take the chest. I will write you a receipt."

"Fuck, no! You can't just waltz in here and take my stuff!"

The outburst grabbed the attention of everyone around the cooking fire. Sweetbread's nephew and son-in-law stood. The guards reached for their swords. One bore a steel one instead of the wooden one the Kingdom used in tournaments. Newman stepped forward to stand with his host's men.

"Please, Sweetbread." Stitches put her hand on the man's chest and stood tiptoe to whisper in his ear. "You'll get it back, it's just temporary. Just go along for a couple of days until people calm down. The guards have orders. Royal orders. You don't want to push them. Please."

Sweetbread glared at the guards. They met his gaze without flinching. He stepped back. "Fine. I want a list of everything on that receipt."

"Of course, of course." Stitches took a fresh sheet and wrote a detailed list of the chest's contents. "Here."

Sweetbread read it over. "Fine."

The guards hefted the chest between them and led the way out of the household's encampment.

Sweetbread took the spatula from his wife, Tightseam, and went back to tending the scramble.

"I didn't think the crown had that kind of authority," said Newman.

Tightseam answered, "They didn't, until we approved them taking emergency action at this morning's meeting."

"I thought Sharpquill had better sense then to pull this kind of shit," muttered Sweetbread. "Otherwise I wouldn't have been an 'aye' for it."

"I think he does," said Goldenrod. "Did you notice Stitches kept saying it was a royal order? And she and the guards are part of the

Kingdom royal court, not the Autocrat's event staff. Stitches does all the Queen's dirty work."

Pinecone said, "If the king's being the problem we just have to wait until the next Crown Tourney. That's what, two months?"

"Back home, yes." Sweetbread stirred the scramble some more. "Who knows when they'll schedule one here?"

"Oh, well," said Pernach, "like I always say, I don't care who the king is, I can always stay drunk for six months."

"No you can't," said his wife. "They took the booze."

Newman walked out of the fire's circle of light and faced the woods. After a few minutes Goldenrod came up and put an arm around him.

"You okay?" she asked.

"A little shook," he admitted. "I was ready to pitch into a fight with two armed men. And I can't honestly say what they were doing was wrong. Last thing we need around here is panicking drunks. But Sweetbread let us sleep in his tent, he's feeding us, he's a friend, so I'm taking his side."

Goldenrod hugged him. "Feudalism is catching."

***

The hunters set out in the morning.

Bodkin and his followers were chatterboxes. Newman didn't want to tell them how to run their hunt—he was the stranger here—but any prey would hear them coming. The conversation focused on archery. Bow-making, fletching, techniques for precision shooting. Newman contributed anecdotes about crafting his composite bow and Boy Scout tournaments he'd competed in.

He realized they were all target shooters, not hunters.

The woods were mixed density. Bodkin led them through a gap in the trees that might be a game trail, if there were big moose here. The undergrowth to the sides had enough room for humans to slip through. Thick patches of shrubs were scattered about separated from each other by dozens of yards.

Droppings and half-eaten leaves were more common in the denser areas. The herbivores didn't like being seen. A scattering of bones, some broken open to yield brains or marrow, showed they had reason.

Which made following this gap a lousy way to find them. But Bodkin and his friends could walk two or three abreast as they chatted.

Newman drifted to the rear of the group. The conversation continued without him. After another ten minutes of strolling he thought he heard rustling off to the right. Without a sound he pivoted into the denser woods.

Walking quietly was something he'd practiced many times. Put his feet on dirt and live roots, not dead sticks or leaves. Go through the empty spots. When a branch has to be pushed aside hold it until it's back in its original position. Keep a steady pace so breathing isn't loud.

A soft grunt ahead was just loud enough to hear. Newman steered to the right of it. If he couldn't hit one he wanted to flush the game toward Bodkin.

Circling a pile of brambles gave him a glimpse of the animals. Half a dozen deer clustered around some flowering shrubs.

Newman looked down. He wanted to look like another herbivore, not a predator. If he didn't spook them he had plenty of time to nock an arrow and line up his shot.

Once he looked to aim he'd have to be quick. Staring eyes were a threat. The deer would bolt.

He chose the nearest as his target. The arrow flew into the deer's belly. It bawled and the rest scattered. By the time he had a second arrow nocked there wasn't a single deer in sight.

Speed won over stealth as Newman chased the wounded deer. At first he ran in the direction he'd seen it go. Then the blood trail appeared. Running must have widened the wound.

He heard the deer before he saw it, panting on the other side of a bramble thicket. Light steps let him see the animal without spooking it. Newman stopped when he could see the rear half.

The haunches were trembling. The arrow had worked deeper into the deer's gut. That meant torn intestines. Gutting it would be messier than usual.

Newman put a second arrow into the meaty haunch. The deer bounded off, wounded leg dragging.

He walked after it. No need to look for the blood trail. Broken branches and the sound of it breaking through brush led him to it.

More sounds distracted him from the pursuit. Bodkin and his friends were calling, "Hello! Newman! Where are you? Are you okay?"

Newman called back, "Over here!" and kept after the deer.

He found it hiding by a shrub again, front legs kneeling. When it heard him the deer struggled to its feet then collapsed.

Newman hung his bow on a branch. His combat knife slid out of its sheath.

He stepped toward the deer. "Shhh. It'll be over soon. Shhh."

The dying animal thrashed. Sharp hooves swung through the air.

A sidestep and pivot kept him clear of the hooves. One quick thrust with the knife to its neck made the deer shudder and go limp. "There. All done."

With the deer silent the commotion from Bodkin and the rest sounded loud in the quiet woods.

"Over here!" yelled Newman. He repeated the shout until the rest of the hunting party staggered into the clearing.

"My God, that's nearly as big as I am!" exclaimed Merrybrew.

The rest were equally impressed.

"Any of you ever gut a deer?" asked Newman.

When they all shook their heads he gave a brief summary of the process.

"Okay," broke in Bodkin. "Merrybrew and Beargut, cut a stick long enough to carry the body with. You two, get the deer hung from a branch. Newman, I need a moment with you."

They walked twenty yards into the woods. A bramble patch seemed to give him enough privacy. Bodkin said, "Dude, you're an awesome hunter. We never saw anything but birds and squirrels and you took down a deer. That's going to feed a lot of people."

Newman waited for the criticism.

"But, dude, we had no clue where you were. You just vanished on us. For all we knew you could have been eaten by a grue. You have to tell people you're going to do stuff like that."

Bodkin seemed to want an answer to that.

"I didn't want to interrupt the conversation," said Newman.

"Well, okay, I appreciate you being polite, but tell me when you're going off on your own. Everything we were saying could wait."

"All right."

Bodkin wanted more.

"I'll keep you informed," said Newman.

"Thank you. Now, come teach us how to gut a deer."

***

"Now I know some of you can't help looking for spinnables," said Mistress Seamchecker, "but food must come first. Look for edible leaves, stems, and especially seeds. Talk to each other. We don't want a dozen of the same plant. We want every different plant."

Eight women held baskets as they listened to her. The gatherers had climbed down the bluff into the flood plain. The meadow here looked much more diverse than the forest above. The plants were a jumble of sizes and colors. *One of them had to be edible, right?* thought Goldenrod.

If not they'd starve.

Goldenrod was in her simplest dress. She expected her knees to wear holes in it before they were done. Her basket was the largest one in the line. Was she being optimistic, or just foolish? She wished she knew.

Seamchecker waved them into the meadow. The line spread a bit, each woman walking a few steps until she saw something interesting.

A weed with wide leaves went into Goldenrod's basket. She wiggled the stems on a yellow-flowered plant and decided it was too fibrous to bother with. The woman to her left collected one of them anyway.

Slapping her arm just smeared the drop of blood. The biting insect had already flown away. "I hope you're allergic to me and die, bug," she muttered.

"This isn't worth it," snarled Mistress Filigree on Goldenrod's right. The bugs found her very tasty. "It's just a waste of time."

"No, we'll find something. I'm sure of it," said Goldenrod. She realized she wasn't trying to convince herself. She had faith that the search would pay off.

Straightening up she saw the gatherers had spread from the bluff to the riverbank. There didn't seem to be any pattern in how the plants were arranged. Floods must have thrown their seeds about chaotically.

Mistress Filigree was complaining again. Bending over to examine plants aggravated her arthritis. Goldenrod walked forward to escape her. A blue-flowered stalk went into the basket, more for its looks than any likely food value.

A white flower with a red center caught her eye. It sprung from a vine, one clinging so close to the ground she couldn't have tripped on it. More flowers showed where the vine disappeared into a stand of thin-bladed grass.

Goldenrod crawled along the vine, heedless of the dirt being ground into her dress. Seven feet later she found where it emerged. Her eating-knife served as a trowel.

The knife loosened dirt, but she needed to scoop it away with her hands. Two nails broke by the time she had one end of the tuber uncovered. It was rooted too well to yank out, but more work with the knife fixed that.

Once freed the root took both hands to lift into the air. Half the gatherers stopped to stare.

"Bless you, child," said Mistress Seamchecker. "How big is that?"

Goldenrod hefted it as she stood. "Maybe fifteen or twenty pounds."

"Goodness. I hope it's edible. Wash it off and go cook it."

The other gatherers examined the flowers to know what to look for. After rinsing the root in the river Goldenrod headed back to camp.

***

Newman walked last in the line of hunters, glancing back every few steps. As they approached the camp cheers broke out. "They got a deer!" cried a herald at full volume.

The animal hung from a roughly trimmed sapling. Beargut and Merrybrew held the ends on their shoulders. They'd already gutted and drained it under Newman's direction. People speculated how many meals it would make.

A man with a grey goatee examined a leg. "It's not a deer."

"Looks like a deer, Parchment," retorted one of the load-bearing hunters.

Parchment bent a hoof toward him. "Look. Three-part hoof. Deer have two toes. This is not a deer."

"It has four legs and antlers. That's close enough. Who cares about the exact species?"

"If it's not a deer," Parchment said with exaggerated patience, "We can't be sure it's safe to eat."

"You think it's poisonous?" asked the other load-bearer.

"Maybe. Or we could be allergic."

The crowd stopped pressing so hard around the hunters.

"It has to be good. We need the food," someone muttered.

"We'll have a few volunteers eat some," said Parchment. "If they feel fine a day later then people can eat the rest."

Some of the crowd drifted away. More volunteered. Parchment winnowed them down to the healthiest young adults. "Only those suited to survive some food poisoning," he said.

Bodkin, the lead hunter, interrupted the selection. "Not Newman."

"I earned a piece of it," protested Newman.

"That's why you'll not be part of the experiment. Two hits with two shots is too much skill to risk."

"Skillful indeed," another voice broke in. "I must bring him to Their Majesty's attention."

"My Lord Autocrat!" Bodkin bowed, followed by the rest.

“I came to offer Their Majesty’s congratulations. You are the first hunting party to catch an animal.” After a few more compliments he listened to Parchment’s 24-hour experiment plan and blessed it.

“My lord?” said Newman as the Autocrat began to turn away.

“Yes?”

“My lord, there’s predators out there. Big ones.”

“Did you see one?” Autocrat Sharpquill studied the other hunters, who seemed almost as surprised as the rest of the crowd.

“Saw piles of bones, sir. Sometimes three-four skulls in a pile. Takes pack hunters to catch that many at once. Lots of cracked bones. They’ve got to have muscle to break them like that.”

“Did the rest of you see these piles?” asked the Autocrat.

“Aye, milord,” said Bodkin. “He pointed them out to us, just like he said. I hadn’t realized the implications.”

“Thank you,” he said. “Runner!”

A ten-year-old boy abandoned the stick he'd been poking an anthill with and ran to the Autocrat’s side.

“My compliments to Master Chisel, and tell him I approve his plan for a palisade. He is to present the details at court.” The boy waved and dashed off.

***

Newman built a fire in the pit while Goldenrod looked through the pots and pans. House Applesmile’s heads were in a big meeting of nobles called by the Autocrat. She felt certain they wouldn’t mind her borrowing what she needed.

A baking sheet and carving knife offered the simplest cooking method for the tuber. She spread half-inch thick slices evenly across the sheet. Newman had the metal rack assembled over the fire. Goldenrod placed the sheet on top.

Strongarm ambled up. “You people are cooking dinner already?”

“Don’t know yet,” said Goldenrod. “It’s an experiment.”

“You’re risking potatoes on a new recipe?”

“It’s not a potato. Don’t have a name for it yet.”

"She discovered a local plant that might be edible," said Newman. If his girlfriend wasn't willing to brag he'd do it for her.

"Oh, wow. That could save our butts."

"Maybe," said Goldenrod. She flipped over some of the slices. They still had the slightly translucent look of the raw pieces.

"Do you need a taste tester?" asked Strongarm.

"Didn't you get breakfast?" said Newman.

"Technically, yes, but you wouldn't believe the rationing Wolfhead Alpha came up with. He wants us to go a month on three days' food."

That brought a laugh from the other two.

"Look, can I try some of the raw slices? Some foods are better raw."

"And some are toxic." Goldenrod pulled up her sleeve. A raw slice of tuber was tied to the inside of her forearm by a ribbon. She slid it over to examine the skin underneath.

"I'm not reacting to it. I guess a small piece wouldn't be too dangerous." Goldenrod chopped another slice and offered it to him on the knife.

Strongarm took it as one bite. The couple watched his face as the fighter thoroughly chewed the slice then swallowed. "Kinda bitter. But I've had worse."

"I just realized the problem with using you as a guinea pig," said Goldenrod. "If you start foaming at the mouth and collapse I'm going to think you're play-acting until rigor sets in."

"I wouldn't do that to you." He chuckled. "Okay, I'd try it on someone gullible." He looked at Newman. "Maybe I could've freaked you out."

"Dude, you set off my bullshit detector in your sleep."

Goldenrod flipped the slices again. "I think this one might be ready to eat. But I'll give it a little more to be safe."

"Anyway, if I'm not poisoned I don't have anything to worry about, right?"

"Depends how well you chewed it," said Newman. "My three-year-old nephew ate a handful of peanuts. But his system couldn't digest them. So that night he's passing chunks of peanuts—with corners."

Goldenrod and Strongarm flinched.

"Well, hey, I'm not hungry any more. So I am digesting whatever that is."

That started a discussion on what to call the tuber. Strongarm's contribution was a Monty Python song, cut short by threat of violence. Goldenrod settled on "vineroot."

Newman ate a slice browned on the edges. "Tastes like a turnip. With a bitter aftertaste. Not hard to chew."

"Cooking softened it then," said Strongarm.

He began another attempt to convince Newman of the joys of armored sword fighting. Goldenrod contributed some stories from crown tournaments she'd watched. Newman listened without reaction.

Strongarm broke off in mid-sentence. "Where's the privy?"

Newman pointed to the corner of House Applesmile's tent.

The fighter dashed off. The house camped close by a portapotty to, as the housemaster put it, make the middle of the night easier.

The portapotty was close enough for Newman and Goldenrod to hear the sounds of Strongarm's distress.

"I think we need to not eat it raw," said Newman.

"I might give some to Lady Burnout as medicine. How are you feeling?"

"Just fine. Ready for another slice."

Strongarm moaned.

***

Many days' march across the forest, farther than any human had yet explored, stood an elven village. One young elf felt the magical chime which meant his master wanted his presence.

Ithuil the apprentice flinched as he saw the opening of the great hollow tree. The rotten trunk should have collapsed long ago. It stood as grim testimony to the power of the magic practiced within. A score of elves could dance inside the hollow trunk. Right now it just held one.

The sorcerer.

Moss and weeds gave way to bare dirt as the apprentice drew closer. Nothing could grow close to the sorcerer's lair. Even the nearest trees were dying.

Again, Ithuil regretted his desire to learn the deep magics.

At the opening his throat spasmed, silencing the apprentice as he tried to utter the proper greeting. He flung himself onto his face on the hard-packed dirt floor.

"You're late. You must hurry when I summon you." The sorcerer's tone was light and cheerful. The apprentice relaxed. He wouldn't die today.

Sandals slapped the floor as the sorcerer walked across. "Into the middle now. I'm going to show you some scrying. One of those bits of bait I set out was nibbled on. I want to see what came through."

Ithuil wiggled forward, not daring to lift his face from the floor. It made a shallow bowl. Pewter-gray toes tapped his nose to stop him before the center.

"Leave room for the puddle."

The apprentice twisted to reach the flake of obsidian tucked into his belt. He slashed his forearm, letting blood pour onto the floor.

"Good."

The blood flowed to the center then started to swirl as magic pulled harder on it than gravity.

"Enough."

Ithuil pressed on the slash to stop the bleeding, hurting himself more than the blade had. He snuck a bit of magic while his master was distracted, knitting closed the blood vessels and skin.

"Watch the hands, boy."

He lifted his eyes. The foot was still by his face, flawless shining gray skin over bones and tendons. Nearly reaching it was the edge of the leather vest, mystic symbols burned black into it. White hair hung to the knees, eddying in the puffs of air displaced by the magic working.

He managed the courage to look higher. The hands were moving in intricate patterns, steering the magic as it formed the blood into a smooth circle. Above them, eight feet off the floor, was the sorcerer's face. Majestic and knowledgeable, it was everything the face of the oldest and wisest and most feared elf in his world should be.

Ithuil gulped and focused on the hands.

The pattern they traced became clear after many repetitions. The puddle of blood spread wider and thinner. Then it became a window looking down on a forest from above.

"Ah, there they are," said the sorcerer. "Frantic as a kicked ant hill."

Ithuil saw the camp at the top of the bluff but didn't recognize the tents as shelters. "They're short. And weak. And ugly," he said.

"All true," said the sorcerer. "But they're tool users. So they may make some progress on the project."

He shifted the view this way and that. Sighed. "Clearly they're not ready. I'll cast a protection on them for now." His eyes descended to Ithuil. "More blood."

***

Morning court opened cheerfully. Newman received three huzzahs for bringing down the deer. The taste-testers had all survived the night. Autocrat Sharpquill then invited Newman to describe the unseen predators of the woods by their effects.

". . . and the long bones were broken to get at the marrow, so they have strong jaws or can use stones as tools," he finished.

The Autocrat thanked him. "Master Chisel has a proposal for building a defensive palisade around our encampment."

The carpenter described a fence of split tree trunks making a U-shape against the bluff, with a gate in the middle.

When the Autocrat asked the populace if they'd be willing to build it today a chorus of "Aye" went up. He declared it an all-hands project for the day. Hunting and gathering were prohibited.

House Applesmile returned to their tent. A quick tool inventory produced a small hatchet intended for splitting pre-cut firewood.

"It'll do," said Newman. He started swinging at the nearest tree.

Mistress Tightseam snapped, "Don't cut that down! It's an oak. We can eat acorns."

"Oh. Sorry." He cast a guilty look at the notch in the bark. It didn't look lethal. He moved to the edge of the grassy area and picked one of the new trees outside the encampment. It looked to be thirty feet tall, though the upper branches wouldn't be useful for the fence. The axe cut into the bark on the side facing Applesmile pavilion.

Pernach objected. "Hey, we want that to fall away from the tent."

"It will. We make a small cut here and a big one on the other side. That lets it fall easier."

"Oh. Didn't know you'd cut down trees before."

"Didn't." Swing. "Watched my uncle do it." Swing. "Of course." Swing. Swing. "He used a chainsaw."

Pernach finished the first cut. The men took turns chopping at the tree, each handing the axe on when his arm hurt too much to keep swinging.

An hour later Pinecone offered the hatchet to Sweetbread only be told, "Give me a minute."

Pinecone dropped it in the pile of woodchips. He flopped down in the grass next to the other men.

Chopping sounded from the neighboring households. Shouts and curses came from the shovel team working their away along the line marked by Master Chisel. The Applesmile women were quietly bickering inside the tent. "No, boiled water in the jug with the blue tape. Red tape is river water."

Goldenrod came out of the tent and surveyed the men without comment. She picked up the hatchet and started swinging.

After a few minutes her swings slowed. When two blows against the trunk produced no chips Newman stood. "My turn, darling."

As he knocked a chip out they heard cries of "timber!" and a crash from their north side.

"Who was that?" asked Pinecone.

Pernach said, "Wolfheads. A dozen heavy fighters should've taken down a tree faster than that."

"Depends what they're using," said a new voice.

Sweetbread pulled himself up. "Your Grace!"

Pinecone and Pernach ducked their heads. Newman stopped chopping and gave their visitor a nod.

The stocky grey haired man carried an axe nearly as tall as he was, bearing a curved blade as long as his arm. "Master Sweetbread, goodmen, morning to you. Give me room, lad, I'm finally getting good use out of this thing."

He swung into the notch they'd cut with so much effort. Splinters and chips sprayed out.

"It's getting dull. I'll be making my third visit to Master Forge soon. Took him half an hour to put a decent edge on it this morning."

Two more swings shook the tree. Leaves drifted down.

"Here, come have a turn with it, boy. See what it's like with a real axe."

Sweetbread hurried to make introductions. "Duke Stonefist, this is my guest, Newman Greenhorn."

"Oh, you poor bastard. The rest of us were just Newman until a new Newman came along. You're going to be stuck with it until someone has a baby!" The duke's laugh was infectious enough even Newman joined in. "Take it, lad. Give it a try."

The first blow taught Newman to blink when he connected. Splinters stuck to the sweat on his face. He hadn't realized how cramped he'd been confined to the hatchet's short arc. This axe let his arms reach out to their full extension. He could put the whole weight of his body behind it.

"Don't steal all the fun, lad, let the others try."

Pernach made chips fly.

Newman watched the duke. Aside from a circlet on his head decorated with gold leaves and a white belt with a fancy buckle he was in peasant clothes. They were filthy with wood splinters, dirt, and soot. Sweat soaked the chest and armpits.

Stonefist made Pernach hand the axe to Pinecone before the tree came down. "Be light on your feet lad. Don't want the thing landing on your head."

The tree crashed to the ground without injury.

The duke pulled a coiled cord from his belt pouch. "Master Chisel wants the poles two feet into the ground and eight above. Scrape here to mark it, lad."

Pinecone made quick work of the top of the tree.

"I'll have that back now. You can handle the rest of this. I'll go help someone else."

They sent Stonefist off with a chorus of thanks.

When he was out of earshot Pernach muttered, "Nice to see one of the hats getting his hands dirty."

"I haven't seen any of the current court breaking a sweat," replied Pinecone.

"Hush, you two," said Sweetbread. "We've work to do."

Newman opened the saw blade on his multitool. It was too short for what they'd been working on but it cut right through the branches on their log.

Sweetbread dropped a handful of tent stakes on the grass with a clatter.

"Doesn't the tent need those?" asked Newman.

"Nah. With no wind blowing four poles are plenty to keep it up. The rest are to keep it steady during a storm." Sweetbread looked at the lighter pavilions of the neighboring households. "Come a storm, I'm going to have a lot of new friends."

"I wonder how bad winter gets here," said Pinecone.

"Not today's problem."

The sledge drove the inch-thick metal stakes into the wood. When one was driven in as far as it would go the next was set at the end of the crack.

"I'm not sure we have enough stakes," said Pernach.

"Oh, it would suck if we can't split this log," replied Pinecone. "There's no way we can pull these stakes back out."

Master Sweetbread growled, "It'll split. Go back along the line and give them all some extra taps."

Newman picked up one of the thicker branches. He sawed off a chunk from the end and began whittling it into a wedge. "We can get the stakes out with this, and maybe force the split some more."

The wooden wedges went into the crack at the base of the trunk. That forced the split through the tree. More blows with the sledge drove the split along the length until the log fell into two pieces.

Goldenrod and Redinkle interrupted their gloating. "Drink, you. You're all getting dehydrated. Should know better."

"Don't want to waste water," muttered Pernach.

"The river has plenty."

"Hauling it and boiling it isn't easy."

"Drink it anyway."

The man obeyed.

Turning the two half-logs into quarter-logs was easier. Sweetbread declared those were the size Master Chisel was looking for. The top half of the trunk made a fifth piece for the fence once they stripped off the branches and peak.

"The tops are supposed to be held together by rope," said Sweetbread. "That's going to use up a lot of our cord."

"We can make rope out of duct tape," said Pinecone.

Pernach objected, "We can't waste tape for that! We'll be fixing everything with it."

"Let me try something." Newman slid a knife blade under the bark on one of the split pieces. He moved along the edge, producing a strip an inch wide and ten feet long.

"Bark is brittle," said Sweetbread.

"The outer bark is brittle. Inner has flex." Newman ran the back of the blade against the strip. Grey bark flaked off, leaving a green ribbon.

Sweetbread felt the end of it. "That we can work with. We'll need to braid it."

"Hoy, make way!"

The shovel crew was getting close. House Applesmile cleared the wood from the marked path. Then they stood back to stay clear of the dirt flung by the shoveler.

***

Newman chewed his bite of roast venison slowly. Rain pounded on the roof of the pavilion. He'd go hunting in a drizzle but there wasn't any point to it in this downpour. He couldn't see far enough to shoot anything.

His stomach wanted the whole bite now. Newman did his best to stretch it out. Sweetbread only carved three ounce chunks off the roast. With no idea how long the rain would last the household's food was being rationed.

The royal decrees issued since their arrival commanded everyone to not waste calories on unnecessary activity. So calisthenics were out as a way to pass the time. Newman was helping Goldenrod with her embroidery project, passing her a new spool of thread whenever she changed colors.

Sunlight penetrated the white canvas of the pavilion. On a sunny day the inside was well-lit as a good workroom. Today the rainclouds left it gray but there was still enough light to see by inside.

Subtle color differences were hard to make out in the gloom.

"This is tan, I need light brown," snapped Goldenrod. She shoved the spool back at Newman.

He set his jaw and silently offered up his second guess. She took it with a grunted thanks.

Normally Newman would go for a walk when he felt this cranky. Slogging through the mud now wouldn't improve his mood. This was the third time he'd held back from responding to one of her remarks. He didn't want an argument. Nobody else wanted to listen to it either. Sweetbread had already stomped on some bickering between Shellbutton and Pinecone.

Eight people didn't crowd a tent this big . . . until no one could escape it.

Goldenrod left her needle stuck in the fabric as she rubbed the back of her neck. "I'm sorry. I have such a headache. I shouldn't be so bitchy."

Mistress Tightseam looked up from her knitting. "When did you have your last soda?"

"Um, day before yesterday I guess?"

"Caffeine withdrawal. Unpleasant, but it'll pass."

"Oh." Goldenrod looked down at Newman. "Sorry."

He smiled. His hands mimed a neck rub.

She shook her head. "Thanks, though."

There wasn't really room to do massage anyway. They'd have to rearrange all the gear dragged in from outside to let people sleep.

A gust lifted the roof of the pavilion. Ropes creaked as they pulled taut.

Sweetbread stood up. "I don't like that wind. Pass me the long rope."

Redinkle produced the coil from a corner. Sweetbread unrolled it. He tossed the middle up several times. Finally it caught on a hook hanging from the ridgepole. The switched-off battery lantern dangling from the hook swayed as the rope brushed it.

"Pernach, Newman, take the corners."

Newman moved to where he was pointed.

When the storm began they'd staked down the walls. Two tent stakes had been kept aside. Now Sweetbread tossed them to the younger men.

Pernach pounded his stake into place. To Newman's relief the three pound sledgehammer was passed hand to hand across the tent instead of being tossed.

Once both stakes were placed Sweetbread flicked the ends of the rope to them. "Tie 'em off. Not too tight. Just enough to keep it taut."

Newman realized why they were doing this. The edges of the roof were held down by rope, but the center just had the weight of the ridgepole holding it down. Now the rope would add more tension.

The rain kept pouring.

***

Goldenrod led Redinkle and Shellbutton into the chiurgeon's tent. It was packed solid. The air was hot with too many bodies in too small a space. The trio sat at Lady Burnout's feet. There wasn't any place else to go.

The messenger had asked for them by name and not said the purpose of the meeting. Goldenrod scanned the faces she could see from her position. All female, and none over thirty.

A few more women came in on the other side, squeezing the standers closer together.

"That's all we're going to get, I guess," said Lady Burnout. "I don't want to give this speech again, so you pass it along to anyone who missed the meeting."

The whispers in the back died down.

"We're in a disaster," continued Burnout. "A slow motion one, but we're going to lose people. We need to bust our butts to make sure we don't all die." She paused.

"There's certain psychological reactions that kick in during disasters. One is pairing up. There's already gossip about that happening. No shame, it's normal.

"The next is having babies. Some on purpose, some because you're too infatuated to think about consequences. More because there's no way to get birth control refills in the wilderness."

That sparked some nervous chuckles.

"Now. I will take it as a personal favor if nine months from now I'm not running from tent to tent trying to deliver twelve babies at once. You will want to have your babies some time when you can have my whole attention."

A short haired woman stood up, pulling her friend up with her. "Then we don't need to be here."

"Sit down, Carnation," snapped Burnout. "My pediatrician friends have dealt with plenty of lesbian parents."

They sat.

"So. If you have pills, keep taking them. Same with caps and cups and whatever. Condoms—the day of single use condoms is over. Wash them—very gently—and let them dry unrolled. Test them by filling them with water and looking for drips."

That produced a few "ewwws" from the back.

"Next option. The rhythm method. Don't laugh, it works if you do it right. Peak fertility is two weeks after the start of your period. Keep your legs crossed three days on either side to be safe. If you've been on the pill you'll need a couple months to establish a pattern after you run out, sometimes longer. Talk to me about it if your cycle isn't regular."

Burnout waited for a few grumbles to die down.

"Yes, the boys will get cranky. Hand jobs and blow jobs. They work. Normally I'd suggest breaking up with him if he's being a jackass but I know there's not many extra men out there."

"What about anal sex?" someone asked.

Lady Burnout shrugged. "It's an option. But we're not getting more lubricant delivered, and we don't have easy hot water. So hygiene's an issue. It'll be worse when we run out of soap."

"What happens when we run out of tampons?" came a wail from a girl sitting on the examining table.

"Not my department," said Burnout.

Goldenrod popped up. "Ragbag," she said. "Sew a little pillowcase, stuff it with cattail fluff, or, well, we'll find something." She sat back down.

"Thank you. Work together ladies, we all have something to contribute. Now I'll let you go."

The crowd streamed out, seeking cool air. Goldenrod hung back. "My lady?"

Lady Burnout lifted her eyebrows.

"Mistress Filigree had three homebirths. I think she knows some of the theory of midwifery too."

"Yes, I talked to her already. But don't tell the youngsters. I want them scared."

***

"Toss me the soap!" called Pernach.

Redinkle was more relieved than annoyed to hear her husband's voice. "Where have you been all day? And go get it yourself. You know where it is."

Pernach stayed in the lane between tents. "You don't want me in the tent. We were conscripted for privy detail. We need a bath."

Behind him Pinecone nodded in agreement.

"A bath wouldn't hurt you either," said Goldenrod to Newman.

He looked at the blood staining his clothes from butchering the deer, or near-deer, or whatever they were going to call it. "Right."

Going down the bluff reminded him he wasn't used to operating in rough terrain any more. Broken plants showed where other people lost their footing and slid down. His legs were feeling the effort after hiking for miles with the hunting party. The other two didn't seem bothered.

"You're enjoying this," Newman said.

"Hell, yeah. I'm not hauling a sixty gallon tank of shit around," answered Pernach.

"Or having the Royal Guards hassle us," agreed Pinecone.

"Guards?"

Pernach skirted a patch where the path was trampled into mud. "Eight of us on the detail. Six of the Queen's Royal Guards to protect us. Not doing any of the work."

"Spearpoint pitched in with the carrying when we slipped," offered Pinecone.

"Until his sergeant told him to stop."

Pinecone held out a steadying hand when Newman reached the steepest part. "At least they didn't hit either of us."

Newman stopped walking. "The guards were hitting people?"

"Just that guy Stonebridge," said Pernach. "He was slacking."

"Damn. Did the guards threaten you?"

"No . . . but I made sure they could see me working hard."

The bluff flattened out into a smooth flood plain. A brief walk brought them to the river bank. Signs were up with arrows marking upstream for drawing water, downstream for bathing and dumping trash. Another said, "Wading only—No Swimming." A two foot length of purple tentacle was nailed to it.

Newman pointed to some guys splashing water on themselves among a few rocks. "That looks like a safe spot."

***

Mistress Seamchecker had been thrilled with the taste of the cooked vineroot slices. As they walked back to House Applesmile, Goldenrod brainstormed with Newman on experiments for planting and cultivating the vegetable.

"Good day, Master Orrery," said Goldenrod.

"Hello, my dear. How are you?" Orrery cocked an eye at Newman. Goldenrod performed introductions.

The craftsman was interrogating Newman about the construction of his bow when shouting broke out.

"Hey, look at that one! It's not a bird, it's a plane."

"No, it's Superman," someone quipped.

"It is a plane. It's flying in a straight line. There's a city out there!" said a third.

Orrery ducked into his tent, emerging with a massive set of non-medieval binoculars. It only took him a moment to spot the object the crowd was pointing at. He twitched.

"Goldenrod, my dear, please tell me what you see." He passed her the binoculars.

She needed a bit longer to find it. She handed the binoculars to Newman without a sound.

Newman didn't have any trouble focusing in. They were similar to field glasses he'd used in the Army.

The object had looked like a plane to his naked eye—a black cross, wings rigid. Magnified the body was reptilian. A trickle of smoke trailed from one of the oversized nostrils. The bat-like wings flapped once then went stiff again.

Newman lowered the binoculars. "It's a dragon."

Goldenrod and Orrery sighed in relief at his confirmation. The craftsman took them back for another look. "Yes, looks like a dragon to me too. Hell of a place we've landed in."

He let some others take turns to confirm it. A few who'd hoped for rescue wept. Most took it calmly.

The least calm reaction was a motherly rant. "No, you're not. One, it would eat you. Two, we can't eat gold. Three, you have work to do here."

***

Master Sweetbread made an experiment for dinner. Mashed vineroot baked with diced sausage mixed in. House Applesmile unanimously declared it a success.

Pinecone was scraping the burnt bits off the bottom of the pot when Lady Stitches arrived, four men in armor at her heels.

"What do you want, my lady?" asked Master Sweetbread. "I promise you I haven't brewed any beer since we arrived."

Stitches' face was flushed with embarrassment. She read off the paper in her hand. "By royal decree, all feminine sanitary supplies in excess of three day's personal use are to be turned in for redistribution."

"Seriously?" demanded Goldenrod.

"I have the order from Their Majesties' own lips."

"This is bullshit," she said.

Stitches' frown grew deeper. "I have been authorized to search your belongings."

Redinkle said, "Fine."

She emerged from the tent with a box of tampons and emptied half of it into the guard's sack. "That's keeping three days' worth."

Goldenrod and Shellbutton made their contributions next.

Stitches turned to Tightseam. "And you, Mistress?"

"You're six years too late for that, girl," she snapped.

The lady in waiting blushed. "Thank you all."

The group marched off.

No one spoke until shouting broke out in the neighboring Wolf Heads encampment.

"I guess Queen Camellia forgot to pack supplies," said Goldenrod.

Redinkle turned to Tightseam. "Mom, I didn't think you'd hit menopause yet."

"Hush, dear. I didn't but there's no need for the Court to know."

Chuckles ran around the cookfire.

"Does the emergency rule really mean the king has the authority to confiscate everyone's property?" asked Newman.

"Aye," said Sweetbread. "The populace cheered a blank check. Besides, under normal law the Crown can decree any laws or actions it cares to."

"No checks or balances at all? How'd the Kingdom last so long like that?"

"Oh, we have checks." Sweetbread settled into his story-telling slouch. "First off that monarchs only reign for six months at a time. And there's no way to predict who'll be next. So that's an incentive to not make rules they'd have to live under.

"Second restraint is tradition. If all your friends give you dirty looks for changing things you don't change much.

"Third is that the Kingdom takes effort to visit. If the King takes the fun out of things nobody shows up the next weekend. Then bards sing about the King of the Empty Hall."

One of the odd native birds went 'cough-cough' on the ridgepole of their tent.

"None of that applies right now, of course. What we still have is peer pressure, trying to convince them that something is unwise."

"Which works better if you're a Peer," quipped Redinkle.

"Fortunately for you you're descended from a pair of them."

"Peers are former kings and queens?" asked Newman. The lecture he'd received on the drive down hadn't stuck very well.

Goldenrod answered, "Yes. Plus the knights, and master organizers, and master crafters."

"Which is where Tightseam and I come in," said Sweetbread. "There needs to be a meeting of the Crafter Council."

"Talk to them about guards hitting the privy cleaners," said Pinecone.

***

"You wished an audience with me, my lord Autocrat?" King Ironhelm let the flap fall shut behind him as he entered Autocrat's tent.

"Your Visiting Majesty, thank you for allowing me to see you." Autocrat Sharpquill waved his staffers out. They exited through the other side, leaving their chalk slates and abaci behind.

Ironhelm took a seat without waiting for permission. The pretense that he outranked the man in charge of food distribution was good for something. The message—effectively a summons—hadn't included a reason for the meeting. The monarch waited.

"Your Majesty. I must beg you to not disrupt the peace of this Kingdom."

This again. Ironhelm didn't let his reaction show. "How so?"

"You're subverting the food distribution plans."

"The giving of alms is a royal duty." Not that King Estoc and Queen Camellia practiced much charity.

"That is so. But we're in a survival situation here. We need everyone working to their utmost, not hanging around begging."

'Everyone' did not include royals or their courts. There'd been pointed complaints from the Court when Ironhelm and his two squires pitched in on the fence building.

"I have not encouraged anyone to beg. We simply pass our excess along to the needy."

"There should not be so much excess for you to give away. You and yours receive the same ration as everyone else in Court."

Which was half again what everyone not in Court was receiving. Some of the gatherers were passing food to King Ironhelm and Queen Dahlia because they didn't trust the Autocrat's system to get it where it was needed. Protecting them was another duty.

"We eat sparingly. It's not like we're manual laborers needing to keep our strength up. And my wife and her ladies sometimes find something when on their constitutionals."

Sharpquill smiled. "Of course. It's the distribution that's the real problem. People hanging around waiting for you to show up at the common pavilion or Chiurgeon's tent or wherever, when they should be working."

Ironhelm thought it would be easier to keep people working if they were compensated instead of conscripted, but it wasn't his Kingdom.

"I was asked to not distribute alms after the official dinner. So we found other times and places."

"We've set up a bonus program giving extra food to those who've earned it through hard labor or taking on dirty jobs. It would be best if your excess was donated to that."

Rumor had it that bonuses only went to those who'd made conspicuous displays of their loyalty to the Crown.

"Best. If I spoke to Their Majesties, would they think it was best?"

"It was Queen Camellia's suggestion."

"Then do you think it is best?"

"Of course. It is Her Majesty's wish."

"No. Not what you think as an officer. Do you, as your own man, think that it is best to stop me from giving alms, and have all food distribution going through one man's hands?"

"Yes, I do. I trust Her Majesty's wisdom in all things."

My God, he believes that. What the hell is going on with him? "Very well. My Queen's ladies in waiting will deliver the excess as needed."

King Ironhelm left the tent. Duke Stonefist had a story of Master Sharpquill telling then-King Stonefist to back off on exercising his royal prerogatives when he became rude. He needed to talk to Stonefist and find out what changed.

***

"No, we're not going to have a meeting," declared Mistress Seamchecker.

Sweetbread was too surprised to reply at once. The head of the Crafters Order had always loved excuses to gather the members before. "There's things we need to talk about."

"We don't need to talk. We need to work. Everyone's busting their asses to help us survive. This is no time to be gabbing in a nice shady tent."

Council meetings were under a seal of secrecy. Standing in the lane as others walked by was an invitation to eavesdropping. Sweetbread tried to pick words that wouldn't disrespect the Crown.

"Allocating resources and making decisions is part of that."

Seamchecker said, "The Autocrat is doing a good job of that."

"It's not the Autocrat I'm worried about."

Mistress Seamchecker shifted from impatient to stern. "Well, *Master* Sweetbread, I suggest you find better things to worry about. Their Royal Majesties told me not to waste time with meetings. So you should work on cooking those new plants people are finding. Good day, sir."

She walked off.

One Week After Arrival

"What the hell have you been doing now?" cried Redinkle as her husband came around the neighboring tent.

Newman grabbed the first aid kit. When he realized Pernach and Pinecone were walking normally he put it back down. He eyed them warily. Both looked like they'd been pulled from a burning Humvee.

"New jobs!" announced Pernach. "No more dirty privy detail for us. We're Master Forge's newest apprentices."

"I've seen boys pump the bellows all day without getting that sooty," she said.

"Well, we're not on the bellows. He's running low on fuel so we're making charcoal. It's a smoky job."

Both young men had patches of black all over them. Even the palest spots were gray with soot, except where sweat had washed a line through it.

"Well, you smell better. Kinda like a grilled chicken."

"Thanks. Can we have the soap?"

Tightseam broke into the conversation. "No. We don't have enough soap for you to use it every day. Just go rinse yourself."

"That's what I did," said Newman. "When we butchered the near-deer today we stripped down to keep our clothes clean."

Pinecone quipped, "Wow. When the soap runs out we'll have a bunch of suicides."

Shellbutton had leaned toward him to get a kiss without smudging herself. Now she slapped him. "That's not funny!" She burst into tears and ran into the tent.

"What?" Pinecone looked stunned.

"You didn't hear Lady Purplebow killed herself yesterday?" snarled Tightseam.

"Oh. No. How'd that happen?"

Purplebow had taught Shellbutton how to make the notions which gave the young woman her name.

"Opened her medicine chest and swallowed it all. Shellbutton's taking it hard, so have some kindness. Now go rinse!"

***

The birds were coughing again. They were used to humans blundering through their woods now. Or Newman had taught Deadeye and Beargut to walk quietly enough to not frighten them.

The trio of hunters were walking down one of the wide paths. That was a poor way to find game but the fastest way to travel. Newman wanted to hunt farther out from the Kingdom's camp. Once they'd covered about three miles he'd take them off the path to look for near-deer.

A flurry of wings told of birds taking off over the path ahead. Then a branch snapped.

Newman pivoted left, waving for the others to follow him.

"What's going on?" asked Deadeye.

Newman whispered, "Something's coming. Get into cover."

Twenty yards into the woods he found a thick stand of brambles. He circled around and took a knee.

Deadeye kneeled next to him. Beargut scuffed some dead branches aside with his boot, making Newman flinch at the noise. The chubby hunter flopped down on his back.

More branches were breaking. A low rumble resolved into a mix of thumps. A "huff" had to be a breath from some big animal. All the noises kept getting louder.

Deadeye let out a low whistle.

"Shhh." Newman raised his head enough to peek through the brambles. He nearly let out a sound himself.

He'd seen rhinos in zoos. This beast had a rhino shape but had to be twice the mass of any Newman had seen before. The stiff hide was covered with long red-brown hair. There were two horns on its nose, but side-by-side in a V-shape.

When Deadeye started to say something Newman put a finger across his lips. The hunter jerked his head away with a silent glare.

As the first rhino moved past they could see it was male. Three smaller females followed it. The middle one had a hornless calf with her.

Once the rhinos were out of sight and the birds returned Newman stood up. "Okay, we can relax now."

"Why are you so afraid of them?" demanded Deadeye.

"Rhinos are nasty. I don't want one of those horns up my ass."

Beargut laughed. "I'm with you."

"Seriously," said Deadeye. "We're out here to hunt. That's an herbivore. We should have taken one down and seen if it's edible."

"Take one down?" Newman pulled an arrow from his quiver. "Do you really think this would go through the hide of one of those monsters?"

"I bet it would hurt the baby."

"Maybe it would. And then its momma and daddy would trample everything in sight. Do me a favor. If you shoot a rhino wait until I'm a couple miles away."

"And don't ask me to carry it back to camp," said Beargut. "The deer are heavy enough."

Newman said, "Yes, they are. Let's go get one."

***

Autocrat Sharpquill stepped into the common pavilion. His staff would bring him meals at his desk every day if he let them. He'd decided to have at least two meals a week in the commons. It kept him from working until he fell over. It gave the populace a chance to talk to him outside Court. And it was a quality control check on the cooking.

The dinner rush was over. The tables were half full. No Peers were in sight. The commons served those with no household or groups not able to gather any food of their own.

The line for the serving tables was short. Though several people were standing around holding empty plates and mugs.

Sharpquill walked toward the line. Halfway there he stopped.

The last person in line was Belladonna.

The one in front of her was facing forward, back stiff, not acknowledging anyone was behind her.

Anyone getting into line could have Belladonna turn and speak to him. Hence the scattering of people waiting for someone else to join the line first.

Doing unpleasant things for the common good was the Autocrat's job. He walked to the end of the line. But left two empty spots between himself and Belladonna, lest she feel an invitation.

She didn't turn around.

Sharpquill studied her back. He'd heard all the rumors. Most took it as given that their arrival here was her fault. He'd confronted her in her tent, chasing out the rest of the household for privacy, but she'd refused to say anything to him. Nor had she admitted anything about causing it to any of the other people who'd asked. Most only received cold silence. Possibly just as well.

What would he do if she said, "Yes, I did it"?

There was no Kingdom law against practicing magic. Kidnapping would be a stretch. And how would they punish her? Hard labor was everyone's lot now.

He could have her burnt at the stake. Some people muttered about that already. But Sharpquill didn't want the precedent.

Establishing her guilt and not punishing her would be worst. A mob would extract its own idea of justice. God only knew if he could regain control afterwards.

Better to leave the doubt.

Belladonna reached the serving table. The server placed a pinch of wild greens on her plate. The previous customers had received smiles and a bit of chatter. For Belladonna the server acted as if the plate was floating in the air by itself.

A spoonful of mashed vineroot was delivered in equal silence.

Lady Buttercup was the last server, holding a set of tongs over a platter of fried fish. When Belladonna arrived Buttercup tucked the tongs into her armpit to free her hands. She pivoted her chair and rolled a few yards back to the cooking tables.

There she found a piece of fish overcooked to nearly burnt. She picked it up with the tongs, held the tongs firmly in her armpit, and wheeled back to the serving table.

The scorched fish landed on Belladonna's plate without a word.

She left the tent to eat alone elsewhere.

Autocrat Sharpquill stepped up to the serving table once she'd left.

"Some greens, my lord?"

"Yes, thank you."

The next server said, "They're mashed today. Tastier that way, I think."

"Thank you very much."

"Here's a nice juicy piece of fish for you, my lord."

"Thank you, Lady Buttercup."

Sharpquill looked for a table with some people he hadn't talked to recently. He found some of the best information in those casual chats.

He wondered if burning at the stake might have been kinder than ostracism.

***

Whatever it was, it was too loud to be a near-deer.

Newman nocked an arrow and shifted left, seeking an open patch in the woods to give a clear line of fire.

The other hunters followed him, not wanting to be left behind. The rustling and snapping made them nervous.

He found a view from fifteen yards away. There was a near-deer, a dead one. Five wolves—more or less—clustered around the kill, bolting chunks of meat. One snarled as a second one stuck his nose under the ribcage.

Newman yelled, "Haroo!" and kicked a branch toward them with a rattle of wood and dead leaves.

The wolves whirled to face him. Growls filled the air.

Newman strode forward, kicking the branch again. "Haroo! Haroo!"

Each wolf ripped a gobbet from the carcass and trotted off.

As the last grey tail vanished among the trees the other hunters crept up.

"So that's what's been leaving those bones we've seen," said Bodkin.

Newman shook his head. "Not all of them. Probably not most of them."

"But they're predators."

"Not the apex predator. They're used to being driven off a kill."

Beargut asked, "The dragon?"

"No. Prey's too small and it can't fit through the trees. There's something else out there."

***

Redinkle pulled open the tent flap. "Hey, come see the rhinos!"

The members of House Applesmile surged out. Newman was last. He'd grabbed his bow and quiver.

"This way." She led them to the bluff. More people of the Kingdom were lining the edge, pointing across the river. "See them?"

A red-furred bull rhino led four cows and a couple of calves through the flood plain on the other side of the river. They were spread out, selecting specific bushes and devouring them in one or two bites.

Newman slung his weapons. "Oh, you worried me. I thought we might have some walking through the camp."

Master Sweetbread laughed. "Don't say such things. The Autocrat will make us rebuild the wall even stronger."

"I don't think we *can* make a wall that holds up to that," said Pinecone.

Strongarm slid over from the Wolfhead group. "Stone walls can stop anything, man. We need a castle."

Something streaked through the air, too fast to make out. Then the black dragon snapped out its wings wide as it slammed into the spine of a cow rhino in the middle of the group. The stricken beast let out a deep moan, loud even across the river. The rest of the herbivores scattered.

Newman threw himself flat.

The bull didn't bother with pawing the ground or other posturing. It charged at the dragon. The winged lizard flapped its wings, rising up to let the rhino pass harmlessly under it.

Goldenrod looked down at Newman in concern.

"Get down!" he snarled. "Do you want that thing to see us? We'd be like popcorn for it. Get down!" The last was shouted for everyone on the bluff to hear.

Goldenrod laid down next to him. The other members of House Applesmile followed more slowly. Sweetbread was stiffest.

The bull rhino slowed and turned about. The dragon landed on the cow and bit at her neck, releasing a spray of blood. The bull bellowed, putting the other cows and calves into motion, and charged again.

"Sir?" called Strongarm.

"Wolves, hit the deck!" ordered Wolfhead Alpha. His warband went prone. Others on the bluff followed their example.

The dragon lifted into the air again. As the bull rhino passed under it, the monster let out a stream of fire. His fur turned black as it burned. The bull continued until clear of the dragon. He rolled twice across the ground then stood, some smoke still trailing from his fur.

The dragon landed on its kill. Teeth and claws pulled up a piece of hide. Once a corner was loose the dragon bit down hard and peeled the whole section away. It breathed flame onto the exposed meat and began to eat.

All the rhino cows and calves were on the downstream side of the dragon now with their bull. They'd gathered together while the bull kept the predator distracted. Now they trotted away, the bull at the end of the line.

"Put out the fires!" someone called. Several people dashed into the camp to obey.

After a few bites the dragon flamed its meal again.

More of the audience drifted away. Newman and Strongarm kept watching. In whispers they debated what the weaknesses of the dragon might be.

Another Wolfhead crawled up to Strongarm. The fighter introduced him as Borzhoi.

"We have Master Chisel's permission to use his raft to go scavenge after the dragon leaves. Are you in?"

"Scavenge what?" asked Newman.

"It's not eating the hide. There's probably going to be some meat left. And we can use the bones. We just need to move fast before it spoils." Borzhoi sounded cheerful at the prospect.

Newman wasn't, but he agreed to join them.

The dragon spent less than an hour feeding before flying off. Wolfhead Alpha ordered his scavengers to wait another hour before letting them cross the river.

Newman's archery fame earned him a spot on the first raft over. Borzhoi posted him as a guard while the rest applied their knives to the dead rhino.

There wasn't much to guard against. Even the birds and river creatures seemed to have fled the dragon. Newman walked over to one of the pieces of hide. The dragon had tossed it forty feet from the rest of the carcass. A bush let him prop it upright. He nocked an arrow, drew back to full extension, and loosed it into the hide. The "thock" sound drew the attention of the scavengers.

"Problem?" called Borzhoi.

"No, just checking something," Newman answered. Half the arrowhead was sticking out the other side. He drew his knife to try to work it out without breaking it. "This stuff would make good armor."

***

With the second vineroot she found Goldenrod started saving the bits with roots and sprouts. Just foraging for food would pick this region clean. She wanted agriculture.

No one objected when she claimed a plot of land at the bottom of the bluff a bit upstream from camp. A vineroot had been found there, so the soil was the right type. Clearing it for planting was the hard part.

She used a digging stick Strongarm had carved from his memory of one he'd seen in a museum. A shallow serving spoon was now a trowel. Redinkle used that when she came to help.

The two women would trade off. One broke the ground with the digging stick while the other smashed lumps with the ladle and tossed unwanted plants onto the compost pile.

"How's Pernach holding up?" asked Goldenrod.

"Oh, he loves it," answered Redinkle. "He was always a fantasy novel junkie so someplace with a real dragon is paradise for him. I worry he's going to run off to search for elves and halflings. How's your boyfriend taking it?"

"He's not exactly my boyfriend. I'll say it, he's not denying it, but he's not saying it."

"I thought you two were dating for a while. You were vague on Facebook."

Goldenrod snapped a plant in half before adding it to the compost. "This is our . . . mmm . . fifth date. I figured if he didn't break up with me after a weekend in the Kingdom we'd be official."

"It's been more than a weekend and he hasn't dumped you."

"I know. But he wouldn't walk out in the middle of a date. Not that kind of guy. So we're stuck in this eternal fifth date and I don't know what's going to happen next."

Redinkle smirked as she leaned hard on the digging stick. "How was the third date?"

"You have a dirty mind."

"That's why I married so young. Well?"

"Well . . . neither of us hesitated arranging for the fourth date."

"Aha!" This time the digging stick made a 'klock' sound as she thrust it into the dirt. "Damn, rock."

Both of them worked to dig out the fist-sized stone. Goldenrod flung it toward the river.

"Whether he's your boyfriend or not, how's he handling this disaster?"

Goldenrod grinned. "Struggle for survival in a strange land he's fine with. It's all the customs of the Kingdom he has trouble learning."

"You're dating a survivalist?"

"No. Ex-Army. He was in the combat zone. Twice, I think. Not sure. He doesn't like to talk about it."

Redinkle tried to shove the digging stick in again. Her hands slipped on the shaft. "Trade?"

"Sure." Goldenrod stood up and started stabbing the soil. Redinkle knelt with the ladle.

"So not the kind to panic."

Goldenrod laughed without breaking her rhythm. "Hell, no. That's how I first noticed him. The company was expecting a visit from Corporate. All the managers were in a tizzy, rushing around and arguing. Then a machine caught on fire. Now they were yelling 'Call the fire department' and 'Evacuate the building.' Newman walked over, blasted it with a fire extinguisher, unplugged it, blasted it again, and went back to what he was working on. Never said a word."

"Good guy to have around."

"If he sticks around."

"I haven't noticed him eyeing anyone else. Crap. This one's roots go deep. Poke it some more?"

Goldenrod gave the dirt around the stubborn plant half a dozen stabs. "Try now."

The ladle levered out the whole plant. "Got it."

"Newman won't eye anyone else on a date. It's his duty to pay attention to me, so he does. But at work he notices everybody."

"So it's good you're on a date with him."

"I don't know. Sometimes I feel like a trapped him into being with me and he'd have to chew off a leg to escape."

Redinkle laughed. "Be serious. He's never had it so good. And there's not much competition for you even among the married women. And the single ladies—sheesh. Watching the singles pair up for the disaster makes me glad I'm married."

"I hadn't noticed."

"That's 'cause you never come to the stitch and bitch. You miss all the gossip. Hey, I know. When it's time to plant, invite everybody our age. We'll stand around the edge of the field and put the cuttings in moving inward. It'll be a sowing circle."

Goldenrod kicked dirt in her face.

Spitting out grit didn't keep Redinkle from laughing.

They both looked up as running steps sounded. "Lady Goldenrod?" called the young man. She recognized him as Bellows, an apprentice.

"Yes?" she answered.

"Master Forge presents this to you with his compliments."

She traded him the digging stick for the new tool. The shaft was fresh-carved wood. The hoe blade was at a right angle to it. The neck was twice as thick as the one in her mother's garden shed. The blacksmith didn't have modern steel to work with so it probably needed the extra strength.

"Gimme some room, honey."

Redinkle scrambled aside.

The hoe blade swung into the soil, pulling up a divot. Another swing chopped it in half, and sliced into the soil beneath. A dozen swings later the soil was more finely divided than any other spot in her plot.

She rested it on the ground and took a few deep breaths. "My thanks to Master Forge. Please tell him this is superb work."

"I'll do that, milady. May I keep this for the next one he makes?" The apprentice hefted the digging stick.

She nodded. He sped off.

"I guess you won't need me any more," said Redinkle.

"We're going to take turns. I can't keep that up long without a rest. But it's a much better tool."

She moved to the corner where she'd started breaking ground and went through it again. "So are any of the single girls eyeing Newman?"

"Oh, sure. He's brought in more meat than any other three hunters combined. Right now that's like captain of the football team."

Redinkle let Goldenrod stew for a few moments before continuing.

"But being Little Miss Horticulture makes you head cheerleader, so they're afraid to try."

***

Master Sweetbread thought the rhino meat Newman brought back as his share would be best stewed. He chopped it up and put it in the pot with cubes of vineroot and a pinch of the precious spices. Then it went over the fire to simmer for hours.

By the smell their neighbors the Wolfheads were grilling their share.

Everyone was working on some task around the cookfire. Newman had a dozen leaf-blade arrowheads from Master Forge. Goldenrod fletched the shafts he attached them to. Mistress Tightseam patched ripped clothing.

The sound of tramping feet mixed with jingling metal told of armored men going by. The group stopped in front of the Wolfhead encampment.

Lady Stitches' voice sounded, making an announcement. It wasn't loud enough for anyone in House Applesmile to make out the words. Newman turned to look. The Wolfhead tents blocked his view. A royal guard stood by the corner, wearing full armor.

When Stitches finished everyone started yelling. Pernach stood up to go investigate but Sweetbread waved him back down.

The uproar became even louder. And angrier. Then Wolfhead Alpha's voice cut through it. "Stand down, boys! Stand down!" He repeated it until everyone else was silent. He stopped. After a couple minutes of rustling and clanking the armored royal guards tramped away.

Sweetbread told his young men to let things calm down before bothering anyone for the story.

The story came to them.

Strongarm came around the corner and approached House Applesmile's cooking fire. "May I join you?"

"Pull up a haybale," answered Sweetbread.

One was already close enough. Strongarm sat, putting a bowl beside him.

"So what the hell was all that?" burst out Pernach.

Strongarm took a deep breath. "Their Royal Majesties decreed that rhinos being majestic, their meat shall be for the exclusive use of Their Court."

Reactions ranged from Pinecone's astonished cursing to Tightseam's disappointed sigh. Newman was silent.

"But Lady Stitches graciously allowed three-eighths as a finder's fee."

"Thus averting a riot?" asked Tightseam.

"It pretty much was a riot. Some shoving. A broken chair. The ugly moment was when Borzhoi put his helmet on and a guard drew on him. Not a rattan tourney sword. Steel. Looked sharp, too."

Pinecone gasped. "Damn. What did you do?"

"Nothing. I waited for orders. While holding onto a tent pole I could get out with one yank. I figure seven feet of oak with a blunt spike against two and a half feet of cheap Paki steel is a fair fight."

"And after the fight?" asked Sweetbread. He stirred the stewpot.

"We'd have a dozen dead royal guards, maybe four dead Wolfheads, and war with the crown. The Alpha was right to shut us down."

Pernach said, "But, damn. Taking food off people's tables?"

"Not now," said Tightseam.

Sweetbread tasted his ladle. "This is ready. Let's have it before Stitches drops by to chat."

He gave Strongarm a wary eye. At past Kingdom events he'd fed the young fighter without hesitation. Hospitality was a virtue. But he'd always brought twice as much food as he'd need for a weekend. Now . . .

Strongarm shifted on the bale, opened his mouth, closed it without saying anything.

"I appreciate you inviting me on the scavenger run," Newman said to him.

That put a thoughtful expression on Sweetbread's face. "Would you like to join us for dinner, young man?"

"Yes, my lord, thank you. I've always admired your cooking."

Rhino meat had a strong taste, but no one complained. When the pot cooled fingers went in to collect the last of the broth.

Wolfhead Alpha strolled by with Mistress Vixen on his arm. His eyes met Sweetbread's. A jerk of his chin pointed toward the bluff. Sweetbread stood, offered his arm to Tightseam, and followed.

Clean-up was handled by the younger set, including Strongarm. Once everything was put away, he returned to his encampment to "see what the new marching orders are."

Newman invited Goldenrod out for a walk in the woods. She wasn't surprised—eight people in one tent left little privacy for fooling around—but he didn't seem in a mood for smooches.

Other couples outside the walls were, so they had to wander a while before finding a spot private enough for Newman. He turned and faced her nose to nose.

Goldenrod popped up to kiss him.

"Hey," he said. "Let's get out of here."

She glanced back at the camp. "We are out of there."

"No. I mean, let's go to the mountains."

"Go exploring?"

"No. Well, some. Find a homestead and settle down, just us."

"What?"

Newman spoke low and fast. "The Kingdom is a pressure vessel. It's going to explode. There's going to be blood. When neighbors kill neighbors the grudges last forever. We have to escape while we can."

She stepped back. "Ye gods, you're serious."

"Of course I'm serious. Do you want to wake up in a tent on fire? Shit like that happens in civil wars."

"It won't be that bad. They'll fix things."

"How? All the checks and balances of this government were left behind on Earth. All that's left is people with unlimited power. It's going to their heads."

"Government doesn't work because of rules. It works because people want to make it work. We have good people. I trust them."

Newman was angry. "Those good people let it get bad enough to almost kill people tonight. Will they fix it fast enough to keep someone from getting killed?"

So was she. "Whether they do or not, I'm not leaving. These people are friends. The closest thing I have to a family. I'm staying with them."

He looked at her. Then looked off in the distance. He was thinking of going by himself. The realization terrified her.

"Look," she said. "Be practical. Two people, just with what we can carry? How good a shelter can we build? What happens when we get sick, or hurt? How do we fix metal tools that break? How bad are the winters here?"

Only one moon of the three was up. Its light left the side of Newman's face toward her dark. He still faced the mountains.

"And when the killing begins?" he asked.

Goldenrod tried to imagine it. She knew he didn't need to, he'd been in the middle of worse. "If the Crown executes Master Sweetbread I'll run away with you."

He let out a long sigh. "I can leave before a fight. I can't quit in the middle of one."

"Sweetbread and Wolfhead Alpha are working to prevent that fight right now. Let's help them."

Newman turned toward her and spread his arms. Goldenrod fell into the embrace.

Two Weeks After Arrival

Newman remembered how to make a fire by rubbing sticks together. Or rather he remembered that he'd done it as a Boy Scout. That was enough for him to be dragooned into teaching a class for a half-dozen commoners who hadn't packed matches.

After an hour of trial and error he had some blackened tinder. The students had copied all his mistakes. A couple had quit in frustration, but others took their place. Strongarm confined his heckling to carrying over a stack of firewood "for when you succeed."

Smoke appeared in Newman's tinder. He spun the stick a few more times to heat it then picked up the board to drop the tinder onto the waiting pile of kindling. Some gentle blowing produced an actual flame. As it spread he added some twigs. Some broken sticks went on next. Strongarm offered a split piece of log. Newman put that on the downwind side. When it caught he flopped onto his back.

"It can be done," he proclaimed, drawing applause from the onlookers.

When the worst of the muscle aches faded Newman sat up again. He added a few sticks to keep his demonstration fire going. Then he went around the circle watching everyone else work. Goldenrod didn't need any suggestions. He squatted down next to her friend Redinkle. "Keep the stick turning all the time. If you take a break, even for a moment, it cools off."

"Right," answered Redinkle, "I'll work on that."

He kept going around. A couple had let the tinder fall away from where the drill pressed into the board. He pushed it back into place for them.

Strongarm took over an abandoned set of sticks. Newman made him focus on control instead of force—"Keep the end turning on the same spot, not moving around"—and left him to it.

Goldenrod started the second fire.

"Cheater. Bet your boyfriend gave you extra lessons," snarked Redinkle.

Goldenrod just laughed at her.

The other students eventually ignited kindling or gave up. Redinkle and Strongarm were the last two still trying. When his kindling sprouted flames, she cursed at him. "How the hell did you start it so fast? I've been at this three times longer than you have."

Strongarm showed his palms. "Calluses, sugarpie. I can twirl harder than your pretty pink smooth hands."

"Not so pretty now." She lifted a hand off the stick to show a burst and bleeding blister.

Newman said, "I think you should stop for today. That needs a bandage."

Redinkle glared at him. "No, dammit, I'm going to start this fire."

The tinder, board, stick in her hand, and waiting kindling, twigs, and sticks all burst into flame together. Flames climbed onto Redinkle's sleeves, skirt, and hair.

Newman tackled her, rolling her over in the grass until she wasn't burning. Goldenrod threw a bucket of water onto the fire. "How the hell did that happen?" asked Newman.

"Who cares? She's hurt." Strongarm picked Redinkle up and trotted toward the chiurgeon's tent. As the pain overcame shock she started screaming. Goldenrod followed. Newman only paused to tell an onlooker to put the fires out before chasing them.

One glance was enough for Lady Burnout to tell the patient sitting on her examining table "Off." Strongarm, Newman, Goldenrod, and apprentice chiurgeon Elderberry were all needed to hold Redinkle on the table. "First degree on face and legs. Third degree on hands." She stepped back and thought for a second.

"What are you doing?" said Goldenrod.

"Triage. Will all three of you work to keep her bandages clean?"

"Yes, milady." "Yes'm." "Aye, my lady."

"Then we'll do it. Here, give her this." Burnout handed a scarce hydrocodone pill to Goldenrod.

With a little water and whispers of, "You'll be all right," Goldenrod managed to get the pill down Redinkle's throat.

"Now, boys, this will be the hard part," said Burnout. "I need to remove the damaged tissue, put on some ointment, then bandage her.

That's going to hurt like hell. You have to hold her arms still so I can work on her." They nodded. "Let's do it."

Everyone was relieved when Redinkle passed out.

***

Newman led Constable over to the fire. Six piles of ash surrounded some unburnt firewood. Redinkle's stood out by its flatness. The other fires had still been charred sticks when put out. Hers was pure ash.

"Who started the one that burned her?" asked Constable.

"I don't know. She was working on her own drill, but she couldn't keep it going long enough to heat it up. I tried to get her to give up and try again tomorrow. Then it all just burst into flame, even the wood she wasn't working on." Newman pointed at the ashes of the sticks stacked up to feed the fire after the twigs.

"Anyone mess with her stuff?"

"No. It just went poof."

"Son, you make it sound like it just magically burst into flame, and I don't believe in magic." Constable had retired after thirty years as a cop, and could produce the look when needed.

"Sir, if you don't believe in magic, how do you think we're here?" asked Newman.

***

They waited two more days before asking Redinkle. Lady Burnout came by once a day to apply ointment. "You're a lucky young lady. That's the fastest I've ever seen such burns heal. I think you'll even recover full function in both hands."

"Thanks," said Redinkle.

Newman stepped forward. "Red, while you're awake, could you tell us how it happened again?"

She glanced over his shoulder at Constable. "Like I said before. I said I'd keep trying, I gave the drill an extra hard twist, then the whole stick was burning in my hand. Don't you believe me?"

"I do," said Newman. "Could you try something for me?"

"What?"

He held out a paper receipt from his wallet. "Imagine this bursting into flame."

"You think I burnt myself?"

"I don't know. Let's test it."

"Goddammit." Redinkle glared at the paper. Flames sprung up along the edges. Newman dropped it. It was grey ash before it reached the grass.

"Now I'll believe in magic," said Constable.

***

Pernach wasted no time putting his wife's new power to work. Once Lady Burnout declared Redinkle healed he dragged her out to the clearing in the woods where he and Pinecone had been making charcoal.

"I don't know what you need me for," she complained. "You're burning stuff just fine."

The clearing was covered with stacks of drying wood, ash, bits of charcoal, and wood chips. In the center a pile of dirt fumed.

"It's not fine." Pernach picked up a piece of wood charred on one end. "Our results are uneven. Some of the wood doesn't burn at all. When we open vents to spread the fire we wind up burning it to ash. We're getting a twenty or thirty percent yield. It's cutting into Master Forge's production."

"I can't ignite dirt." Redinkle paced around the edge of the mound.

"It's mostly wood. The dirt is to keep air out so it smolders instead of burns." He crouched, put a hand against the dirt, slid a few feet to the right, and checked again. "Here's a cold spot."

Redinkle pushed her fingers through the layer of dirt and leaves. When she touched split wood she concentrated for a moment. Flames flared from the hole as she yanked her fingers out.

Pernach tossed a shovelful of dirt on the hole. "Perfect. Now I don't have to try venting it."

She was kneeling next to the mound. “I might have made ash of that piece.”

He shrugged. “I’m always going to lose some of it. This is just a matter of balancing the burn. Gotta keep it between wood and ash.”

“Looks like you’re getting a lot of ash.” The floor of the clearing was mostly grey.

“Not that much. The ash stays here. Unburnt wood goes into the next mound. We rake out the charcoal. The dirt and ash goes on top of the next mound.”

Pernach waved at the remains of his previous burn. Flecks of charcoal too little to bother picking up dotted the dirt. Lines from the rake still showed.

“The ash from the cookfires all goes into the dirt too.” Redinkle frowned.

“Yeah.”

“I might have to get a pot and burn some wood to get clean ash.”

“If that’s what you want, talk to Master Forge. He has a metal box for his furnace. What do you need the ash for?”

“If I mix it with meat drippings I can make soap.”

“Is that aimed at me? I swear I’ve been scrubbing hard in the river.”

Redinkle kissed him. “And it’s working. I want it for me. I miss being *clean*.”

***

Two royal guards strolled down the lane past the chiurgeon’s tent. They didn’t seem to be going anywhere in particular. Constable thought they were walking for the joy of seeing everyone else get out of their way.

Every day the Court was more like the dealers and punks he used to arrest. The two guards walked liked thugs newly beaten into a gang and wanting to show off their colors. Constable trailed behind them, waiting for the trouble to start. He’d have to intervene fast if the guards drew their swords. The taller guard carried a wooden tourney sword—

unlikely to kill with a single blow unless it hit the head. The other carried a rapier. The tip gleamed. It was newly sharpened. That could be lethal with one thrust.

A young boy, barely into his teens, crossed the lane without looking around. The short guard, Ranseur, ran forward, slamming his shoulder into the boy's side, flattening him.

"Watch where you're going," snarled the guard.

The victim—Constable recognized him as Sparrow—rolled onto his back and sat up. "What?" He pulled a pair of earbuds out of his ears.

"You're a clumsy fool. You need to stay out of our way."

Constable saw a crowd gathering. More witnesses, good. He just needed them to have the nerve to testify.

"You hit me," complained the boy.

"Get up." The other guard, Bardiche, pulled the boy to his feet.

"Now apologize," said Ranseur.

In normal times Constable would have intervened already. Now he wanted it to escalate to a crime so blatant Their Majesties would have to admit their royal guard was running wild. He kept watching.

"Apologize for what?" stammered Sparrow.

"Apologize for being a stupid, ugly, fool who got in my way." Ranseur poked the boy in the chest.

Not, alas, hard enough to be a felony.

"Hey, he has music playing!" Bardiche grabbed the earbuds from the boy's hand. The cord pulled an iPod out of his sleeve. The guard grabbed it. "It still has charge. It's fully charged!"

"Give that back!" Sparrow's attempt to retrieve his gadget was blocked by Ranseur.

"You have batteries? Where are you hiding them? All batteries were confiscated."

"I don't have a battery, just my iPod. Give it back!"

Ranseur grabbed the boy's chin and pulled him into a nose-to-nose confrontation. "Bullshit. Nothing stays fully charged for three weeks. Where's your juice?"

The boy used both hands to pry the guard's grip off. "Leave me alone!"

The guard pulled his arm free and swung it around for a solid face slap.

His target just squawked.

"His music sucks." Bardiche had an earbud in. He scrolled through the gadget's list.

"Let go!" Sparrow shoved against Ranseur's chest.

The short guard grunted, stiffened, and fell onto his back.

"Hey, what did you do to him?" Bardiche dropped the iPod in the dirt. He grabbed the boy's arm and pulled him around.

This time Constable saw bright white sparks as the boy's hand reached for the guard's chest, accompanied by a popping sound.

The second one fell prone.

The boy stood still, staring at his hands.

Six strides took Constable to the prone guards. The first one to go down was awake, moaning in pain.

"Don't hurt me," said Sparrow.

Constable lowered the head of his mace of office to rest on his boot toe. "I'm not mad at you, son."

He raised his voice. He needed to put the right story in the witness's minds, before somebody gave them another one. "You're the victim here. I saw them assault you and steal your property. I just want to know how it happened."

"I—I don't know."

A friendly smile was Constable's favorite approach now. Be a friend, don't rush him, let the silence push him into talking.

Except there wasn't silence. The crowd was jabbering, witnesses telling the story to new arrivals attracted by the commotion. There was one arrival he was glad to see.

"Where are the casualties?" demanded Lady Burnout. She pushed through the crowd, emerging next to Constable.

"They'll be fine," said Constable.

The two royal guards were acting more hung-over than injured now.

"What happened?" she asked.

Constable said, "I have a theory." He glared at Sparrow.

"I didn't do anything! I didn't hit them, I just touched them!"

The lawman stepped forward, grabbing the teenager's upper arms. "I don't believe you. You set it up with your two friends. They're faking it. Just a big practical joke. I don't think it's funny." He shook Sparrow in rhythm with his words.

The boy's hands on his chest were gentle. The electrical shock wasn't.

Lady Burnout tried to catch Constable as he fell. He was too heavy. She managed to turn him to land on his side instead of the back of his head.

"Augh," he said.

"What did you do to him?" snarled Lady Burnout at the boy.

"I didn't do it!"

Constable recovered faster than the royal guards. "It's all right, son. I apologize. I wanted to test you. You have a strong gift. You just need to learn to use it on purpose instead of in a panic."

Sparrow stared at him in confusion. "What gift?"

"You brought the lightning, lad. Shocked me. And them. You can be gentle with it, that's why your gadget has power. Go home. Think about it. Test what you can do. Go."

A by-stander handed the boy his iPod. He vanished among the tents.

"Lightning?" asked Lady Burnout in a skeptical tone.

"Electricity," answered Constable. "Felt just like the taser hit I took in training."

"Damn fool thing to do with the shape your heart is in."

With her help he stood up. "Weren't you wishing for a defibrillator? I found you one. He'll just need to train up."

She snorted. "That's what, the third one now?"

"The third we've noticed, aye. More useful than the girl who makes birds fly in little circles."

Three Weeks After Arrival

Shellbutton passed out bits of baked vineroot as the members of House Applesmile dressed. No matter how hungry they were at dinner they'd learned to save some for morning so they wouldn't have to work on an empty belly.

"Mandatory populace meeting! All subjects report to court at once! Mandatory populace meeting!" The bellower continued as he walked down the lane, barely audible through the tent wall.

Pinecone asked, "What the hell?"

"I don't know," answered Sweetbread. "Get your shoes on so we can go find out."

Newman hefted his bow. "Should I leave this here? I want to head out for a hunt when this thing is over."

"Bring it. There'll be plenty of swords there."

House Applesmile found themselves stuck behind the Wolfheads. The fighters weren't marching in step but they walked in formation, making it clear they were a unit.

Wolfhead Alpha drifted back until he walked next to Master Sweetbread. "Did you talk to him?"

"Yes. Found him quite sane and sensible for a heavy fighter."

"What did he say about how the Court's acting?"

"Not much. But he's unhappy about it. Being a guest here limits what he can say."

"Guest, hell," muttered Alpha. "We're all permanent residents."

"If we have wide support he'll back us, I'm sure of it. I'll talk to more household heads tonight. Can you sound out the knights? Two or three would be enough."

"Yes." Wolfhead Alpha would have said more but they'd arrived.

The lawn in front of the Court pavilion was packed with people. A few were trickling in, urged on by a royal guard. One man was rubbing his arm.

A herald boomed, "Court shall commence when all are in attendance."

There was thrashing and bumping going on behind them. A man shouted, "Dammit, I was on watch all night, I deserve some sleep! Ow!"

He staggered out of his tent, followed by two royal guards. He joined the crowd without further fuss.

More noise made it clear the royal guards were searching every tent. They found two more night workers and a woman who couldn't walk unassisted. She was carried to Court in a chair.

The monarchs took their seats. Newman noticed the visiting monarchs, Ironhelm and Dahlia, had been shifted to the edge of the pavilion. The space around the ruling monarchs King Estoc and Queen Camellia was filled with gaudy courtiers and half-armored knights.

There was none of the usual ceremony. Autocrat Sharpquill stood forward and reeled off six names to present themselves. Only Thistle the food thief stood.

"I recognize them," said Pernach. "It's all the guys on the shit-hauling detail."

"Thistle! Where are your co-workers?" demanded the Autocrat.

"I don't know. They don't talk to me."

Sharpquill's sternest glare didn't elicit more. He waved Thistle back down. "Does anyone know where Cockleburr is?"

A young woman, plain of face and garb, timidly raised her hand.

"Speak, lass," ordered the Autocrat.

She stood. "I don't know about Cockleburr. But last night Sharpaxe told me he and some friends were going off to start a camp of their own. He invited me along but I'm afraid of the woods."

"I'm surprised it took so long," muttered Pernach. Pinecone nodded.

Under pressure from the Autocrat others confessed to seeing the five 'sanitation workers' leave. When the night shift gate guards confirmed seeing the departure the Autocrat snarled, "And you let them?"

"Nobody said not to," said one guard, a Wolfhead named Whippet.

"I thought we were there to keep dangerous stuff out," protested the other.

Some people in the crowd laughed.

Master Sharpquill pivoted to face the center of the crowd. "Anybody who thinks this is funny best stop using the privies. Keeping them clean and empty is the only thing between us and a dysentery epidemic. If that happens we're likely finished. We're still partly living off food we brought with us. If half our people are down sick and the rest tending them we'll starve."

The crowd was silent now.

"Sanitation duty is important. Workers have been evading it by transferring to other jobs. I'm switching them back." The Autocrat pulled a rolled-up paper from his sleeve.

Pernach and Pinecone were the first names called.

Master Forge popped to his feet. "My lord Autocrat, I cannot work steel by burning wood. I need charcoal. Those two are the only two making it."

"Very well." The next two names Sharpquill read produced an explanation from Master Chisel of how the stakes and fittings carved by them were essential for freeing up metal ones for Master Forge to turn into the tools they needed.

So it went with the rest of the Autocrat's list. Every man escaping the privy detail had found a noble protector.

"Dammit, somebody has to do the work," said the exasperated Autocrat.

A voice from the crowd called, "Put the fighters to work. All that standing around playing sentry is a waste of time."

"Mine are working," said Wolfhead Alpha. His voice projected over the crowd without effort. "They're hauling water up the bluff and hunting deer on top of guarding the wall."

Pernach shouted, "Have the royal guard clean the privies. They've watched it done every day, they know how."

The monarchs had been watching without speaking, blessing the Autocrat's actions by their presence without interfering, as was traditional. Now Queen Camellia spoke. "Our Guard is needed to maintain security and order. They cannot be spared for menial tasks."

On their thrones to the side King Ironhelm and Queen Dahlia gazed at her in astonishment. No one gathered around Estoc and Camellia reacted at all.

Autocrat Sharpquill fixed his eyes on Wolfhead Alpha. "The water hauling is appreciated. For the hunting—how many near-deer have the Wolfheads caught?"

"One. They're still learning the trade."

"Indeed. While Newman Greenhorn comes home early every afternoon because he and his companions can only carry so much meat. I hereby declare the Wolfhead hunters apprentices of Newman Greenhorn, to be his load bearers until he declares them fit to hunt on their own."

Newman's attempt to work out the implications of that was shattered by Wolfhead Alpha's bellow.

"Who are you to give us orders!"

Sharpquill was too astonished to respond.

Master Sweetbread muttered, "Dammit, we talked about this, you promised to wait."

"He is my delegate, issuing orders on my behalf," said King Estoc. "The orders he gave you carry my authority."

"Your authority is on Earth!" retorted Wolfhead Alpha. "There's nothing giving you authority here."

The populace all shouted at this. Some declaring his statement treason, rebellion, or some other crime. Many others agreeing, claiming the Crown wasn't valid or had exceeded its authority. Even some of the courtiers shouted back, though Newman couldn't make out what they were saying through the roar.

No one had the nerve to confront Wolfhead Alpha, but people were arguing in the crowd. Some started shoving.

King Estoc rose from his throne and walked into the crowd, lowering the noise as people turned to watch him.

"Silence!" he commanded.

Most obeyed from long habit.

"If the Spring Crown Tourney isn't considered valid by all, then we will have a new tourney. A week from today. This will settle the rule of us all. Until then, follow the Autocrat's orders."

He stalked back to his throne.

The announcement quieted the crowd more thoroughly than the command for silence had. No one seemed to be sure how to respond. The exception was Queen Camellia, who bore a smug smile.

Sharpquill's brief horrified look—understandable to anyone who'd ever planned a tourney on less than three months' notice—was replaced by his usual dour expression. He returned to the initial purpose of the meeting.

"A schedule will be posted for sanitation work. All fit young men not needed on more important work, such as hunters, will have the duty one day a week. You may trade shifts as long as the work gets done."

There were murmurs but no actual objections. The Autocrat went on to list some other task assignments.

"That's an improvement," said Pernach.

Pinecone snapped, "How is us hauling shit again an improvement?"

"If there's fighters on the detail the royal guards won't be so free with their sticks. They were appointed for sucking up to Camellia, not fighting skill, so most of the fighters can kick their ass."

They broke off the conversation as Wolfhead Alpha approached with half a dozen men. "Master Greenhorn," he said with a touch of sarcasm. "Here are your new apprentices."

Newman had no idea how to handle apprentices, so he fell back on old habits. "Welcome. Get your gear, everything you need for a full day in the woods, and meet me outside the gate in twenty minutes."

They responded with a mix of nods and "ayes."

He pointed toward the Wolfhead encampment. "Move!"

They departed at a brisk walk.

Wolfhead Alpha gave Newman an approving nod before letting Master Sweetbread drag him off for a private chat.

Goldenrod whispered in Newman's ear. "Should I offer congratulations or condolences?"

"I'll let you know when I get back tonight."

***

The Wolfheads were chatting with Beargut and Deadeye.

"Yeah, all he lets me do is carry the bodies," said Beargut. "But I get a cut of the meat. And he always gets some meat. Beats hanging around the common pavilion waiting to see what the Autocrat doles out."

Borzhoi noticed Newman approaching. "Good morning!"

"Morning," said Newman. "Form line!"

The Wolfheads formed a line off Borzhoi's left. Deadeye and Beargut took places at the end.

Newman stood in front of Borzhoi. The Wolfhead held his bow out for inspection. Newman ignored it. "Show me your knife."

Extracting the knife from Borzhoi's belt pouch took a few moments. Newman pulled it from the sheath, checked the sharpness, and handed it back. "Find a way to carry it so you can get at it fast. If a predator jumps you there won't be time to nock an arrow. Canteen."

Borzhoi's canteen had a satisfactory heft. His bootsoles had no holes. Newman moved down the line. A couple had plastic water bottles shoved into pockets instead of real canteens. Everyone's blades and footgear were acceptable.

Newman posted to a spot facing the middle of the line. "Food's getting short. Just about all the food we brought with us is gone. We've eaten bare the roots and berries close to camp. The game is getting scared of us.

"So we're going farther out than anyone but the scouts have been. Five or six miles straight out. Then we cast about for prey, take down all the near-deer we can carry, and head home. Can do?"

Borzhoi belted out a hearty "Can do!" Everyone else grunted or mumbled some vague agreement.

Probably the best he could get. "Let's go," said Newman. He led them into the woods.

Rhino trails were the fastest way through the woods. They didn't go the way Newman wanted to but some were close enough to be worth using for a mile or so.

After cutting through some dense woods Newman led his squad out into another rhino trail. They stumbled into the opening with exclamations of relief. He waved to gather them together.

"I know you don't like being assigned as bearers instead of hunters. We're going to take a moment to cover why. Who walks quietest among you?"

The shortest Wolfhead—Husky, if Newman had their names right—raised his hand. "I'm stealthy."

"Okay. See that bramble patch? I want you to walk there and back, quietly as you can. The rest of us will close our eyes and listen." Newman turned his back to the brambles.

Husky wasn't bad for a city boy. Didn't break any branches. Could put his feet on dirt without making a sound. No gear jingling. But that still left a lot of swishing, rustling, and rattling. Newman had no trouble picking up when he turned around at the brambles.

As Husky came closer to the group of hunters he slowed even more to be as quiet as possible. Newman fought down the temptation to turn around and leap at the guy to drive home how noisy he was being.

"I'm back," said Husky.

Newman opened his eyes and turned around. "Okay, good effort. Now it's my turn. Everyone close your eyes again."

Part of Husky's problem was that he'd taken a straight-line path to the brambles. Newman's was more evasive. He looked ahead to make sure he wouldn't find himself forced to step in a drift of leaves or push through brittle branches.

He still reached the brambles in half the time Husky had. "Okay, take a look," he called. Everyone turned around to see him there. Newman didn't want anyone claiming he hadn't gone the whole distance. "Close your eyes again."

When they'd all turned their backs he started moving. Following the same path he'd used before let him move faster. He stopped arm's reach from Borzhoi. "That's how you do it." Louder than necessary.

Borzhoi didn't jump but half the other Wolfheads did.

"Anyone notice a difference?" asked Newman.

Husky said, "You were quieter." He didn't sound resentful, good.

"That's right. And the deer hear better than you do. One bad step and they'll run. We need to sneak up on them. When you can do that you'll be a hunter. Until then you're a bearer. Let's go."

***

Constable quickly closed the tent flap behind him as he entered Lady Burnout's pavilion. Rain dripped from his cloak onto the rug.

"Wish I could offer you some tea," said Burnout. It wasn't much warmer in her pavilion than outside and Constable looked cold.

"I'm fine. I was at Sharpquill's and he has a fire going." Constable said that with a sarcastic lilt. Few people in camp received a large enough wood ration to use it for heating as well as cooking. They were all in the Royal Court or among its favorites.

"Hmph. So what's the news?"

"No trouble for Sparrow over zapping the guards. The witnesses agree they had it coming."

Lady Burnout sighed in relief. "Good. Are those two being kicked off the Royal Guard?"

"No. Queen Camellia likes them too much. Sharpquill was surprised I even asked."

That drew a rude noise from his hostess.

Constable continued, "Sparrow is being put to work. Lots of gadgets need to be charged. That makes him part of the Autocrat's staff."

"Good. That's probably as safe as the boy can be."

"Sharpquill wants us to figure out what's going on with the magic."

Burnout threw her hands in the air. "How the hell should I know? Nothing makes sense here."

"We have some data. Let's see what we can make of it." Constable hung his cloak from a hook then sat in a wicker chair.

Burnout pulled a folding chair around to face him. "What data? Some mysterious force yanked us here. Now random people have random powers."

"I don't think it's random. All three were panicking over something and now they can do magic for whatever scared them. Marjoram was up a tree taking eggs out of a nest. The parents started clawing her, she nearly lost her grip and fell. Now she can control birds."

Constable ticked the examples off on his fingers.

"Redinkle was failing at firemaking. She got upset. Maybe that was more angry than scared, but anger usually has fear under it. Her power is starting fires."

Third finger. "Now there's Sparrow. Two big guys threaten to beat the crap out of him. Bam. He's taser-boy."

Burnout interjected, "Doesn't explain how he could charge his iPod."

"Well . . . he's into his tunes. We're all under stress. If the music stopped at a bad time he could have panicked."

She considered. "That fits. But it's reaching."

"We have a hypothesis we can test. Strong emotion lets people tap into magical abilities. Whenever new powers pop up we ask them how it happened."

"How does Belladonna fit into this?"

Constable thought for a moment. "I don't think she does. She cast her spell back on Earth. All the witnesses I've talked to say she was perfectly calm."

"The description Elderberry gave me agrees. Have you gotten anything from Belladonna herself?"

He shook his head. "She won't talk to me. Have you tried?"

"I've tried. But she just turned and walked away. I want to give her a follow-up exam but she won't have it. I'd think with everyone ignoring her she'd be desperate for someone to talk to."

The retired cop shrugged. "Some people break in solitary. Others like the peace."

A thoughtful minute went by.

Burnout broke the silence. "Here's the problem with your hypothesis. Not enough magic users. We're all stressed. Most of us are scared as hell. We've had three suicides. If panicking was enough to bring out magical ability half the camp would be levitating or making rabbits appear."

"That's . . . huh. You're right. Maybe . . . it only manifests if there's a problem you can solve with magic?"

"How can you test that?"

"Can't, really, until we know what magic can and can't do. And we haven't even started on that."

Constable stared at the single candle lighting the pavilion. "Or . . ." he continued, "There could be people with magic we don't know about. Too subtle for anyone to notice. Or might discover a power and hide it from everyone."

"Why hide it?" asked Burnout.

"Depends on what it is. I'd be creeped out if someone raises the dead."

***

Strongarm walked with an odd limp as he approached. Newman could tell it wasn't a knee or ankle injury. Strongarm's gambeson was spotted with sweat and creased where steel armor had been strapped on. He must have just finished fighter practice.

"Lady Goldenrod," he began, "would you have any bruise cream? The Wolfheads are all out." He accompanied this with a bow, less graceful than his usual little flourish.

"A little," answered Goldenrod. "We've been using it for sore muscles. How bad do you need it?"

"King Ironhelm kicked my ass at practice."

Goldenrod chuckled and ducked into the pavilion.

"I thought kicking wasn't allowed in heavy fighting," said Newman.

"It's not. Remember how I wrapped my sword around to hit you in the back of your head? Ironhelm did that to my ass."

"Ouch." Newman tried to put more sympathy than amusement into the comment.

"All part of the game. Oh, thank you," he said as Goldenrod handed him a white tube. "Um, do you mind if I use your tent to, um . . ."

"Go ahead," said Goldenrod. "How much of a turnout was there for the practice?"

Strongarm's voice came clearly through the tent flap. "Maybe a score. Nobody from Court except Ironhelm and his squires. They're not really part of Court anyway. They were romping over everyone. Seems as royalty he's not supposed to do manual labor, but as a guest he's excluded from all the organizing and stuff. So he's just been practicing in armor every day."

"Good," she said. "I'd rather have him than Estoc."

The announcement that the reigning monarch would compete had scandalized some traditionalists, but no one had a good counter to his argument that if he wasn't enough of a monarch to keep reigning he wasn't enough of one to sit out the tournament.

Strongarm said, "Hey, Newman, you should come to practice tomorrow. We could get you authorized and you could fight for Goldenrod in the tourney."

"I have to hunt," said Newman.

"You can take a few hours off. There's other hunters at the practice."

"I'd foul out. My reflexes are all wrong."

"That's what practice is for. We won't have to teach you how to hit, you took me down just fine."

Newman's mouth worked but he didn't say anything.

Goldenrod said, "I don't want to be Queen now. I have enough work to do with my garden."

"And pass up your chance to appoint a Royal Gardener?" quipped Strongarm. "Oh, that's better." He emerged from the tent still adjusting his gambeson.

"Going to get a decent night's sleep this time?" asked Goldenrod with a smirk.

"Well, that's not just up to me."

"There you are!"

Newman looked up at the shout. The young woman was familiar, he thought she was a member of the Wolfheads.

Strongarm spoke to her in his sweetest tones. "My lovely Foxglove! I was going to come see you as soon as I finished post-practice maintenance."

"Maintenance?" Foxglove glowered at Goldenrod.

Goldenrod side-stepped to stand next to Newman, who obediently put a proprietary arm around her shoulders. Foxglove turned her glare back on Strongarm.

"Did you file your intent?" she demanded.

"Not yet. It's a big decision." Strongarm waved his hands in what he hoped would be a soothing way.

"We decided it last night."

"Well, we discussed it."

"We did more than discuss!"

Newman wondered if the Kingdom was old-fashioned enough for breach of promise suits, or if the trial would be by gossip.

Either way Strongarm yielded.

"Yes, you'll be my consort. I'll file intent for us at practice tomorrow."

Now Foxglove was smiling. But before she could reward him with a kiss a new voice interrupted.

"No, you won't." None of them had noticed Wolfhead Alpha walking up.

"What?" said Strongarm.

"You will not compete in Crown. No Wolfhead will."

"You can't order us—"

"Listen. The tourney committee decided King Estoc won't be part of the double-elimination tourney. He's just going to fight the winner. So we can't tire out the contender or Estoc walks away with it."

Goldenrod burst out, "But Duke Stonefist is on the committee! How could he let them get away with that?"

Wolfhead Alpha's tone was grim. "Stonefist voted for it along with the rest. Along with the rule that they're not required to call blows. It can go until one is knocked cold."

Goldenrod, Foxglove, and Strongarm all gasped at that.

"So we'll put our faith in King Ironhelm. Strongarm, you need to bring up twenty gallons, I don't care if you make one trip or four. And you—" He turned to Foxglove.

"I'll get back to the kitchen," she said.

When the Wolfheads were all gone Newman said, "That's it? All the talk of tyranny and revolution becomes we watch a duel between two men and hope the new one wins?"

"Choosing a monarch by combat is the tradition of the Kingdom," answered Goldenrod. "Usually it works well. And if Estoc wins nothing changes, we can keep pushing back like we had been."

"If he wins, it changes things. He has more legitimacy. And he's smoked out his opposition, he can take action about that."

Goldenrod had no answer.

Wanting to lighten the mood, Newman asked, "Why were you talking about Strongarm getting a good night's sleep?"

She laughed. "Two Crown tourneys ago Strongarm made it to the sixth round. Impressed a lot of people. So last time he was considered a possible winner. Long-shot, but it happens sometimes. The night before, depending on who you listen to, his consort wanted to make him very motivated to win or he was taking advantage of her wanting to be queen. He showed up in the morning totally exhausted, had no sleep, and went zero for two. I don't think Marigold's spoken to him since."

"Heh. Yeah, I can see her being pissed. But that, and how Foxglove was talking, makes it sound . . . transactional."

Goldenrod shrugged. "Most contenders fight for a spouse or lover. Or friend. Some knights will pick consorts who've worked Court so they'll have someone to handle the ruling aspects. And others . . ."

She blushed. "There are ladies who'd do things for a chance of being queen they wouldn't do for a million dollars. And men like Strongarm who'll make the trade. It's a powerful title."

Three Days Later

"Hey, I see something orange," said Husky.

When he pointed they could all see it. The neon shade stood out against the forest greens and browns.

It was a pop-up tent, before it was torn open. The owner picked a good camping spot on a small hill. The crest diverted most runoff from the flat rise the tent was set up on.

Two tents, once they counted the pieces.

Which was easier than counting the bodies. They'd had the flesh stripped off but enough bits of muscle and gristle clung to the bones to keep them from matching the medical displays Newman had seen.

"Found a skull," said Beargut. "Well—half a skull."

Toothmarks showed on the remnant of nose. Big pointy teeth. Could be a wolf. The face had been chewed off. Not enough left to identify him.

Newman picked up the skull with a scrap of tent fabric. The back of the head was missing. Bugs flew out as he tilted it. The breaks in the bone were jagged, no tooth marks. Maybe bashed against a rock? He was standing next to an outcropping that would do the job, but any evidence had been washed away by the rain.

He turned it to look inside. Blood and goo smeared the skull. It looked like a batter bowl after his mom let him clean it. His stomach lurched. No, the marks were probably made by a scavenger's tongue, not fingers. Newman stayed silent. The Kingdom had enough troubles without starting a cannibalism rumor.

"Damn, this rib cage is empty," said Husky.

Newman took a look at it. "Probably some little scavengers came by later." He squatted down to take a closer look. One rib was broken and shoved out of position. "This wasn't done by a bite."

Borzhoi looked over his shoulder. "Knife?"

"No cut mark on the other rib. Spear, maybe."

"Could have gotten into a fight with each other," speculated Borzhoi. "Then last one ran off."

Beargut asked, "Figure these are the shit-shovelers who deserted?"

"No one else is missing," said Newman.

"Found the fifth skull," called Husky.

"That's all of them," said Newman. "Let's get them gathered up."

"Like hell!" said Deadeye. "I'm not touching any of it."

"They're people. Our people. They deserve a funeral." Newman projected for the whole group to hear.

"I'm not picking up any bones," said Deadeye.

Borzhoi stepped between them. "Look, let's just pile up the bones and put rocks over them. Say a few words. Have a funeral here."

Newman waved the Wolfhead aside. Deadeye had never liked following Newman's directions. Even after the Autocrat made the lead hunter position official Deadeye kept resisting or evading orders. Newman walked up to the other man, leaning in to go nose to nose.

"These are human beings. They deserve a real funeral. With lots of people attending." Newman put a harsh tone in his voice. "You will help make that happen."

Deadeye pulled his knife from its belt sheath. Beargut and the Wolfheads stepped back.

Newman kept his gaze locked on Deadeye.

After a long, tense moment the archer stepped back and looked down. "Okay, okay, have it your way."

"Let's use those pieces of the tents as bags. Should be enough to carry all the bones." Newman set an example by scooping some finger bones onto a yard-long piece.

Husky found a net laundry bag among the camp debris which worked well for the larger bones. There was a shortage of extremities, likely carried off by scavengers. Most of the squad was diligent enough to finish quickly despite Deadeye and a couple of others slacking.

Newman made three loops around the hill looking for more bones or signs of which predator killed the runaways. All he found was sodden clothing blown off the hill by last night's storm.

A couple of improvised bags had to be consolidated to keep small bones from leaking out. When everything was secure Newman shouldered the laundry bag and led them back toward camp.

He spent the hike composing an apology to Goldenrod.

***

The doorway of Autocrat Sharpquill's tent was a small opening where the corner of one of the canvas walls was hooked up to open a wedge. It didn't invite anyone without proper business to enter.

The teenager stooped to peek through. "My Lord Autocrat?" he said softly.

The Autocrat looked up from the table he was working at. "Yes? Ah, Sparrow. Come in."

The boy ducked through. He took a smartphone and a laptop from a sack. "I've charged your batteries, milord."

"Excellent." He shoved some slates aside to make room, making a clatter as they bumped into others.

Sparrow put the gadgets down, nodded, and fled.

"Let's see if they still work." Sharpquill picked up his phone. It made the normal chimes as it booted up.

"Can't see what you want that for," said Lady Cinnamon. "Now this will be useful." She opened the laptop and pressed the power button.

Sharpquill smiled. "Let's see."

When the phone was ready he opened the book reader app. Searching on 'survival manual' brought up seven books. Most showed the "0%" of ones bought on sale and downloaded but never read.

He handed the phone to Countess Fennel. "Your excellency, please go through these and see if there's anything helpful for us."

Cinnamon stacked up several slates and leaned one against them. She started typing the notes chalked on it.

***

Autocrat Sharpquill gave permission to bury the bones. They went next to the graves of the three suicides, against the bluff a bit downstream from the camp.

Wolfhead Alpha found the shovels and broke ground. Enough volunteers came forward they could dig in frantic bursts and trade off as they flagged.

The hunters rested, weary from forcing the pace through the woods. Goldenrod accepted Newman's apology. She claimed she hadn't imagined that level of danger.

A crowd grew a stone's throw from the grave, all those too weak or tired to wield a shovel. Only those who'd done some work stood close enough to supervise the digging.

A tall white-haired man holding a worn Bible approached Wolfhead Alpha. "Good day. I'd like to say a few words, unless someone else . . . ?"

"No, Lord Pulpit, I'm glad you're here. I'd meant to send for you but I was focused on—" He waved at the grave.

"Of course. I'll begin when you're done filling it back in."

"Thank you."

Some of the diggers were willing to go until they reached bedrock but at five feet the soil was wet enough they began to sink. Many hands hauled them out.

Newman stood and waved to his hunters. They lifted the bags of bones and carried them over. At the grave they paused.

"Just toss them in?" asked Beargut.

"No." Newman handed his bag to a digger then scrambled down the side into the grave. The digger crouched down to hand over the bag. Newman placed it gently into the mud then reached for the next.

By the time all the bones were in the grave he'd sunk to his ankles in the mud. Strongarm and another Wolfhead reached down to pull him out. Newman wiggled his feet to keep the mud from pulling his shoes off.

Filling in the grave was quick. Only two men could stand in the hole to dig, but all four shovels could toss dirt back in.

As dirt mounded up the crowd closed in. Lord Pulpit began singing "Amazing Grace" with five older women. Some of the crowd joined in. More people were picking their way down the bluff toward the funeral. Two more hymns gave the late comers time to join the crowd.

The diggers and hunters had merged into the crowd, leaving the space around the grave empty. Lord Pulpit stood beside it. "The Gospel according to Matthew. The twenty-fifth chapter."

The whole crowd heard him clearly.

"Then shall He say also unto them on the left hand, 'Depart from Me, ye cursed, into everlasting fire prepared for the devil and his angels. For I hungered, and ye gave Me no meat; I was thirsty, and ye gave Me no drink; I was a stranger, and ye took Me not in; naked, and ye clothed Me not; sick and in prison, and ye visited Me not.'

"Then shall they also answer Him, saying, 'Lord, when saw we Thee hungering or athirst or a stranger, or naked or sick or in prison, and did not minister unto Thee?' Then shall He answer them, saying, 'Verily I say unto you, inasmuch as ye did it not to one of the least of these, ye did it not to Me.'"

He closed the Bible. He hadn't looked at it while reciting.

"When these five young men left camp I talked to others about it, but everyone was more interested in the other events of that day. As was I. When we heard of their deaths I realized I didn't know their names.

"I asked dozens of people. They didn't know their names. Even the royal guards who'd kept them at their labor couldn't remember all their names. But I found some who'd supped with them and could tell me: Candlewax, Stonebridge, Pauldron, Cockleburr, and Sharpaxe.

"I asked what their mundane names were, that if we ever return to Earth their families might be informed of their fate. No one knew. I asked the Autocrat for the waivers they signed on arrival." Pulpit waved toward the bluff.

Following the gesture Newman saw two men on the crest above the funeral. One was Master Sharpquill. King Estoc stood beside him, crown glinting in the sun.

"The waivers had been turned over to the court when other paper ran out. These young men carried away the last evidence of their identities. They are strangers now forever.

"They were the least of us."

Lord Pulpit paused for his words to sink in. The crowd was more than half the population of the camp. Few from Court though.

"They were not the only ones conscripted to haul shit."

A stir went through the crowd at the vulgarity in a sermon.

"Yes, shit. Every one of us shit in a bucket those poor boys hauled away. At first there were plenty of hands for the job. But we didn't like our friends hauling shit. We found them better work. Apprenticeships. Guard duty. Food gathering.

"These five kept hauling shit. From dawn to dusk. No friends to talk to, no household to lay their head in. After all, they're new. Why waste effort on making friends with someone new?"

Newman saw some flinching at that. A muscular black man nodded in agreement. Newman was surprised he didn't recognize him. Blacks were rare enough in the Kingdom he thought he'd noticed all of them already. Then he realized it was King Ironhelm without his crown, in a yeoman tunic.

"These, the least of us, labored at the worst duty here, keeping us all healthy. They were not visited, not comforted, barely fed. We abandoned them. So they abandoned us. Would they have done so if they'd known the danger? Perhaps. Perhaps they'd rather die than haul everyone else's shit one more day.

"Now they rest from their labors. We pray that they are at peace, gathered in Lord Jesus's loving embrace.

"Now others are the least of us. Those whose names we do not know, for we look past them. Let us treat them as we would treat our Savior come among us."

He opened the Bible again. "In the sweat of thy face shalt thou eat bread till thou return unto the ground, for out of it wast thou taken; for dust thou art, and unto dust shalt thou return."

Then Lord Pulpit led them in the Lord's Prayer and dismissed them. He led his choir in "Clouds of Witness" as they left.

Four Weeks After Arrival

The only challenger was King Ironhelm. The announcement from the throne that bouts would be fought "until one champion yields or loses consciousness" had gotten rid of everyone seeking to get practice or impress a girl. The break with Kingdom tradition made the populace restive. Ironhelm saw a victory in the dueling ground as the only way to prevent a riot or even open warfare between the pro- and anti-Estoc factions.

They clanked their way onto opposite sides of the grounds. Count Dirk lifted the rope to let Ironhelm in. Was that a sign the officer in charge of martial activity favored the challenger? Or was that reading too much into it? Probably too much. He needed to stop brooding and focus on the fight.

A herald stood in the center. He bowed to the queens on their thrones, then turned to face the populace. "Ladies, lords, and commoners! Behold the tourney for right of sovereignty over the Kingdom! On my left, our reigning monarch, King Estoc, winner of eight championships in the Kingdom, fighting for the glory and honor of his consort, Queen Camellia!"

Cheers rang out from the court and populace, forcing him to pause. Ironhelm studied the crowd. The crown's supporters were packed tightly on that side. His own side was silent, a few hissers quickly shushed by their neighbors.

When they quieted the herald resumed. "On my right, the visiting monarch of a Far Away Kingdom—" The official phrasing brought harsh chuckles from some. His home kingdom was now much farther away than a six hour drive. "—King Ironhelm, winner of nineteen championships and thrice king before, fighting for the glory and honor of his consort, Queen Dahlia!"

The other side cheered, and were met with hisses and boos. Ironhelm worried whether they would accept him if he won, then put it aside. Fighting distracted would guarantee a loss.

The revised protocol skipped the fighters standing side by side to salute the thrones. The courtiers negotiating it seemed to fear treachery. As the herald bowed himself out of the ropes Ironhelm saluted Estoc. The ruler returned it. Their squires fastened on their helms before ducking under the ropes in turn.

"Lay on!" cried Count Dirk.

Ironhelm took a few wary steps forward, studying his opponent. Estoc was younger, faster, and taller. He'd have to find a weakness to win, and he'd never watched the king fight before. A few knights had shared their observations, all variations on "Don't leave any openings, he hits like lightning."

Estoc hadn't moved. Odd, his reputation said he'd be charging in. Ironhelm shifted left four paces. The king only pivoted to watch him.

Trying to provoke a response, Ironhelm rushed four steps forward, then hopped to the side. Estoc only raised his sword to guard position, then lowered it when the threat passed.

If the boy wants to wait, I can wait all day long, thought Ironhelm.

A gentle breeze stirred tent flaps and banners, drowning out the whispers of commoners asking for explanations of the standoff from their older friends.

Estoc let his shield and sword hang down, exposing his whole center. "What are we doing?" he asked quietly.

"What?" replied Ironhelm, watching his opponent for a sudden attack.

"This is stupid. Why are we doing this?"

"Your Majesty, this was your idea."

"It was?" Estoc paused for thought. "It was. Huh. Well, it's still stupid."

Ironhelm kept his guard up in case this was a trick. "So now what?"

"Now I break the news to the ladies." Estoc let his sword dangle from its wrist-strap and shield hang from the elbow loop. That freed both hands to remove his helm. He walked over to the edge of the dueling ground to address Queen Camellia in a low voice.

She smiled and laid her hand on his cheek.

Estoc slapped his helm on without fastening the chinstrap, gripped sword and shield, and charged at Ironhelm. "Die, you bastard!"

Ironhelm twirled left to dodge. His sword parried a blow sneaking around the edge of his shield.

The charge carried Estoc past. He stumbled to a halt. "That's so strange. For a moment I hated you. Now I'm back to normal."

Queen Camellia stood at the ropes. "Fight! Fight hard!" she yelled.

The helm shadowed Estoc's face but the shock of realization showed in his body language, even through the heavy armor. "You! How could you?"

Ironhelm followed the logic. "Keep your helm on," he ordered his fellow king.

Camellia turned to look behind her.

Autocrat Sharpquill came out from his place behind the thrones. "Your Majesties, this tournament must be fought to a conclusion or we will have no resolution of our disputes."

Ironhelm turned to face his squires. "Marshals, knights, and squires! Find all the full helms you can. Place them on the courtiers." Men ran to obey.

Queen Camellia tried to countermand the order but King Estoc endorsed it. Worried discussion among the populace grew loud.

The courtiers submitted to the helms. A few fled in shame. Others burst into apologies or explanations for their recent actions. Sharpquill said only, "That explains the confusion I've been feeling."

The angriest was Lady Stitches, Queen Camellia's chief lady-in-waiting. After taking off the helm she shouted into Camellia's face, "You did that to me? After all I've done for you, all the sacrifices I've made, you made me a puppet? How could you?"

"Please. You're no better than the others," said Camellia. She turned her back.

Lady Stitches' belt held everything needed to swiftly repair damaged garb. The scissors were sharp and needle-pointed. Stitches shoved them into Camellia's neck. The queen collapsed soundlessly.

Guards knocked Stitches to the ground. She didn't resist.

"Chiurgeon!" called Sharpquill. Panicked courtiers flocked around the queen's body.

"I'm here, dammit. Let me through!"

"Make way for Lady Burnout," ordered the Autocrat.

The chiurgeon's examination was brief. "Went in between the second and third cervical vertebrae. Not a damn thing I could do for her, even if we were in my ER." She looked up to see Estoc standing over her. "I'm sorry."

She backed away to let the king embrace his wife's body.

***

"All rise for His Majesty King Estoc." The herald had managed to not say "Their Majesties" this time. The king sat in his throne, nervously glancing at the empty one still next to his. He waved everyone to their seats.

"Does Your Majesty wish to—"

"Just get on with it."

The herald turned toward the populace. "Let the prisoner be brought forth!"

Four guards came in surrounding Lady Stitches.

Autocrat Sharpquill stepped forward. "Lady Stitches, you are charged with the intentional murder of Queen Camellia. How do you plead?"

The accused flashed a smile across the populace. "I will not plead with you. You are no judge, no prosecutor. There's no police here. None of you have any right to put me on trial. As for my actions, I acted to defend myself from an attack worse than murder. I protected all of you as well. You should be thanking me, not imprisoning me." She raised her chin and stared directly at the Autocrat as she finished her speech.

People in the crowd murmured to each other as he weighed his answer. "I have no nation's laws to enforce. I don't know how to run a criminal trial. I don't know how dangerous Queen Camellia was. I don't know how self-defense counts with magic. I don't know where justice lies in this case." He paused. The nobles and populace sat silently.

"You have certainly proved yourself unworthy of the titles you hold. Therefore you are stripped of your court barony, your grant of arms, and your award of arms." He waved to the guards surrounding her. One pulled the circlet off her head, the other cut the cord of an elaborate medallion dangling from her neck.

Lady Stitches smirked victoriously. "So you don't dare give me any real punishment. You admit I was right."

Master Sharpquill's face went red. "I do know that I'm tired of listening to your self-serving rationalizations."

He took three steps toward Stitches. "I sentence you to have your tongue cut out!"

A gasp went through the crowd. Stitches backed away, pressing her body against the guards behind her. King Estoc sat bolt upright on his throne. King Ironhelm leaned toward his queen as she whispered in his ear.

The guard who'd cut off the medallion let it fall to the grass. He swept the dagger he'd cut it with behind him to hide it, then tried to shove it back in the sheath, fumbling and letting it fall. He set his foot over it.

The Autocrat continued, "Sentence suspended on good behavior. If you hurt anyone, steal anything, say anything that pisses me off, then—" His hand reached for her face. The thumb and index finger snapped shut before her mouth.

Stitches cringed, both hands over her mouth.

Autocrat Sharpquill turned and walked back to the thrones. Over his shoulder he said, "The prisoner is dismissed."

The guards stepped back. Stitches fled. The populace parted before her. She disappeared behind a tent.

Sharpquill looked at the herald and snapped his fingers. The functionary cried, "Are there any with business before this court?" A flyer went "cough-cough-cough" in a tree.

The herald turned toward the Autocrat. "Um, does he . . ."

Master Sharpquill glanced at King Estoc.

The shock on the king's face had been replaced with fury.

"His Majesty has nothing to say."

The herald bellowed, "This court is closed. All subjects are free to go about their business." The populace fled. Estoc kept glaring at the

Autocrat. The subject glared in return. Ironhelm grabbed Estoc's shoulder and whispered in his ear. They left, surrounded by courtiers.

Sharpquill looked around. Only the minions charged with cleaning up were left. "Don't let me get in your way, lads." They watched silently as he walked away.

***

King Ironhelm steered Estoc toward the 'visiting royals' pavilion. The younger man was in too much shock to resist. Ironhelm just had to overcome his inertia.

Queen Dahlia took Estoc's other arm. She gently said, "Wait a moment, Your Majesty. Then we can talk."

Lady Cinnamon, their chief lady in waiting, held the tent flap open for them. As the kings and queen went in Ironhelm looked over his shoulder at Lord Joyeuse. "See to it we're not disturbed."

"Aye, sire," answered the squire. He blocked the trailing courtiers from following.

Estoc fell into the folding chair he was steered to. His mouth worked but he still couldn't talk.

Lady Cinnamon pointed at a drawer as she glanced at the queen. Dahlia nodded to her lady in waiting. Cinnamon took out a quarter-full bottle of rum, poured a shot, and brought it to Estoc.

The young king swallowed half, coughed, and choked down the rest. "God. Did you see that? Did that really happen?"

Ironhelm said, "Sharpquill ordered Stitches' tongue cut out. He's threatening to actually do it."

"He did it on my authority. I did it! He didn't ask me, he didn't tell me, he just said it. God. That's horrible. Torture."

"It's period." A wry smile flickered on the older king's face.

"You wouldn't laugh if you were in charge of this mess."

"No, I wouldn't. But in a very real sense you aren't either."

Estoc took a deep breath. "I didn't want to be. I just wanted to give Camellia a fancy party. Oh, God." He buried his face in his hands.

They waited for him to recover. When he straightened up Cinnamon made a handkerchief appear in his hand. He nodded thanks.

"I could fire him. I nearly fired him in Court."

"Yes, you can. Who will you replace him with?"

"I don't know. He was the only guy who applied for the job."

Queen Dahlia said, "Not many people want to spend war weekend working instead of playing. Being in charge of how much food everyone gets—that they'll fight for."

"Yeah."

Cinnamon poured a half-shot into Estoc's glass. The king tossed it down.

"I don't know what to do. What Camellia did to us was bad but she didn't deserve to die for it. And Stitches. I can see executing people for murder. But mutilating them?" Estoc shuddered.

King Ironhelm waited for his fellow king to say something more. When the silence continued he said, "You have three decisions to make."

"Oh God."

The time Ironhelm kept waiting until Estoc couldn't bear the silence.

"Dammit, Camellia made all the decisions. She talked to everybody and researched stuff and, and, and I trusted her. Fine. What's the first one?"

"Will there be any additional punishment or pardon for Stitches?

"No. No. I'm not going to execute her just on my say-so. That would be murder. And I'll be damned if I'll do anything nice for her after what she did to—what she did."

"That's settled then," said Ironhelm. "Next. Do you want to appoint someone else to handle administration of justice?"

"Take it away from Sharpquill? That's a good idea. I could appoint Duke Stonefist. He's a lawyer in mundane life. Everyone respects him. He'd be a good judge. Don't know what I'd call the job though."

"You could let him pick his own title," suggested Queen Dahlia.

"If I do that he'll be the Lord High Executioner." A hint of a smile appeared on Estoc's face for an instant.

"Which might be useful in making some of the boys behave," said Ironhelm. "Most important decision. Are you replacing Master Sharpquill?"

"Damn. I don't know. That's tough."

Dahlia took another turn as good cop. "Break out the pros and cons. What's the good points of keeping him?"

Estoc paused to think. "He's done a good job of holding us together. Everyone's getting at least a little to eat. He's made some bad decisions but some of those were probably because of Camellia's . . . influence."

He accepted a mug of water from Cinnamon. Sipped. "If he stays in place we avoid a shitstorm of drama over his replacement. People wanting the job, not wanting someone else to get the job, knifing each other over the job."

"Does he want to keep the post?" asked Lady Cinnamon.

That surprised Estoc. "Why wouldn't he?"

"The way he was acting in Court just now seemed . . . self-destructive. The rudeness, disrespecting the Crown. The sentence."

Ironhelm sighed. "I didn't want to share this. A few days ago Sharpquill's sleeve slid up and I saw hesitation marks on his arm."

"What marks?" asked Estoc.

Lady Cinnamon answered. "When someone tries to commit suicide by cutting their wrists they make some weak cuts before they actually do it. That leaves shallow cuts, scabbing over, where they hesitated before making the lethal cut. Hesitation marks."

"Oh. I can see that. He misses his wife."

"He's married?" asked Ironhelm.

"Yeah. Or he was. His wife was supposed to bring their two boys here Saturday morning. Guess they're safe back home. But he misses them. I can see losing his wife making a man suicidal," the widower said bitterly.

"Or he could have been trying to escape the mind control," said Dahlia.

"Maybe." Ironhelm shrugged. "How can we know?"

Estoc drank more water. "If he commits suicide I can replace him without it being my fault. But that would still be a shitstorm.

"The real con of him staying is bad decisions. I think he'll do better than anyone else we can put in the job. I'll look for parts of it I can carve out and give to someone else.

"So—I'm keeping him. And I hope he doesn't kill himself."

Ironhelm stood. "It's settled then."

"If we don't want Sharpquill killing himself he needs a hug at least," said Lady Cinnamon.

Dahlia said, "I wouldn't ask that of you."

"Thank you, Your Majesty. But keeping the linchpin of our food supply in working order is in my own self-interest."

"What?" asked Estoc.

"I'm going to go see what I can do for Sharpquill." She lifted the tent flap.

"What if he wants more than a hug?" protested the younger king.

She shrugged, and vanished.

***

A hand tapped on the tent canvas. "My Lord Autocrat? Are you there?"

Sharpquill lifted the flap to see his visitor. "I am. Come in."

"Thank you." Cinnamon, Chief Lady in Waiting of the Visiting Court, swept into the tent. She stood in the middle, studying its neat arrangement by the light of three candles on Sharpquill's desk. The big bed was rumpled on one side. Two small cots were neatly made up.

Sharpquill said, "I presume you have a message from Their Visiting Majesties?"

"No, I'm here on my own business," said Lady Cinnamon. "I am very impressed with how you handled that unpleasantness in court."

"You seem to be the only one."

"Oh, no. You've made it clear murder will be punished."

Sharpquill mimed a pinch at his mouth. "People are attached to their tongues."

"But she's still able to work."

"We need all the hands we have to survive."

"Stitches is terrified you'll carry out the sentence."

He shrugged.

"It seems you only failed in one goal you were trying to achieve."

He stiffened. "Oh?"

Cinnamon leaned in with a smile. "You didn't get the King to fire your ass."

"I will not shirk my duties." He started an angry shout, but muffled the rest lest someone outside hear him.

"We know. Otherwise you would have found another way out." She grabbed his hand and turned it, pushing up his sleeve to show healing cuts leading up from the wrist. Some freshly scabbed over, others nearly invisible now.

He shoved her away. "Let go!"

She landed on the bed, smoothly as if she'd intended him to push her onto it. "Your duties are crushing you."

He turned away and leaned on his desk. "I have to keep working. We can't afford to tie up everyone in leadership arguments again, we've lost enough time to such already."

"Then let me help you."

That drew a bitter laugh. "You want the job? Fine."

"No . . ." She stood and came up behind him, breasts brushing his back. "Help you personally."

He twisted away. "My Lady, I am married!"

Cinnamon locked eyes with him. "You were married. Now you're alone. However we wound up here, we're not going back. You won't see her again."

Sharpquill turned to look at the empty beds. "I think of her every day. Her and our boys."

"I'm sure she thinks of you. But she's had a funeral for you already. We're here now, and we have to take care of each other."

"I miss her," he whispered.

She wrapped her arms around him and pulled him down with her to sit on the bed. He buried his face in her shoulder as the tears came. She rocked him and stroked his hair, saying nothing.

***

"Enough," said the sorcerer.

Ithuil pressed on the cut to stop the blood flow.

"Sit."

The apprentice tilted his body up, kneeling on the dirt floor inside the hollow tree. He studied his master's gestures as the sorcerer transformed the blood into a broad puddle, and then a window to the forest.

The sorcerer exclaimed over the latest developments by his pets with all the excitement of an elfling watching birds build a nest.

Ithuil wasn't close enough to the scrying pool to see what his master was exclaiming about. His attention drifted to the walls.

The inner surface of the trunk was pocked with shelves and cubbyholes carved into the wood, the work of prior generations of apprentices. All of them were full. There were jars and bundles of wild herbs, some collected by Ithuil. Stoppered bottles of potions with cryptic labels no one but the sorcerer understood. Book after book with the sorcerer's records of his experiments. Scrolls with the perfected spells.

"They're ranging widely now. Outside the circle of my protection. Ah, yes. There. Five deaths, oh, a hand of days ago. Eaten, I'd wager. They'd tried to claim land outside their fence. Good. If they're being that bold they'll be effective at exterminating the vermin."

The apprentice flinched at the venom in his master's voice. Attempts to wipe out the menace directly had been . . . costly. Now these strangers from another world would do it.

The sorcerer stepped back from the scrying pool. After a moment's thought he said, "Yes, it's time. They no longer need my protection."

He turned to Ithuil, who flinched and picked up his blade again.

"No, no, this won't need more blood. You will take down the protection spell. It's made from your blood. You should have no difficulty."

A scroll in the middle of a pile wiggled loose and soared into the master's hand. He offered it to Ithuil.

The apprentice forced his hands to not shake as he took it. Other apprentices shared rumors of a scroll that left the caster as dust, a trap set for thieves and nosy apprentices. Another rumor said all the scrolls would dust their readers.

Even if that was true it would be a better end than the punishment he would suffer for defying his master's will.

He read through the whole scroll. It should "Unmake a distant enchantment" as the title claimed, based on the thaumatological theory he'd been taught. The leather of the scroll was still supple. It had been made less than a decade ago.

Staying on his knees he shuffled to the edge of the scrying pool. His right hand hovered just above the surface, as flat as he could hold it.

Scrying wasn't just for sight. Ithuil could hear the murmur of the river. He felt with his magical senses and found the protection spell. It was a sphere centered around the stockade on the bluff. Touching the currents of power in it he confirmed that it was only meant to exclude the green vermin from the protected volume.

He looked back at the scroll. The symbols burned into the leather specified the sounds and gestures needed to unravel the spell. He began the chant. His fingers moved in synchronicity, interlacing then pulling apart, interlacing then pulling apart.

A current pulled loose from the sphere and came to him through the scrying pool. He changed his hands to pulling and guiding. A glance at the scroll verified he was doing it right. As the sphere weakened its power flowed back to him faster. At the end the remaining power rushed into him with such force Ithuil fell onto his side.

"How do you feel?" asked the sorcerer.

From a stew of possibilities he chose, "Warm."

"Yes. That's the magic of your own blood come back to you. A pleasant feeling."

The apprentice rolled onto his back. He saw his master's face above him wearing an unfamiliar expression. Amusement? Happiness? Surely not the latter.

"You did well, Ithuil."

That was not just unfamiliar but unprecedented. Disbelief delayed his response. "Thank you, Master."

Ithuil hoped the delay hadn't been rude.

"You are now a senior apprentice. Stand."

He stood up, half expecting to be clouted back down for his presumption.

"That's enough for today. Alas, it will take another hand of hands of days for the vermin to find their way back to the protected woods. I must be patient. Oh, you may go tell your news to the others." The sorcerer opened his current book and held a needle in a flame.

"Thank you, Master," he said again. He ran from the hollow tree. Who to tell first? Greet the other senior apprentices as an equal? Or gloat in front of the relatives who'd predicted he'd be dead within a year?

One Month After Queen Camellia's Death

Newman was hungry. His breakfast was half the size he was used to. His stomach wanted more.

The rest of his squad looked hungry too. The month since the aborted crown tourney had been hard on everyone.

He gathered them around him rather than making them form a line. "The game's getting scarcer. We have to go farther out to find near-deer. They're in smaller groups when we do find them. Between us and the wolves and whatever the other predators are there's a lot of pressure on them.

"So we need to adapt. Instead of one group with a bunch of bearers we need more hunters and smaller groups. Easiest is to split in two with me and Deadeye as hunters. We'll do that this afternoon."

The squad was waking up. Deadeye liked having his own team. The rest were realizing this wasn't just a pep talk.

"We're going to train you as hunters. Stalking. Tracking. Archery you already know, but we'll work a bit on moving targets. Lesson one is walking without scaring the hell out of the deer."

They'd gone far enough from camp that the woods weren't trampled over. Newman stepped off the rhino trail into the trees.

"Watch my feet as I walk. I'm not going in a straight line. I'm stepping on dirt or moss. Dead leaves and twigs make noise."

He took a few more steps.

"That's a root. I can step on it. It's too solid to crack. Notice how I'm putting my feet down. Gently. I'm walking at normal speed but slowing the foot right before it touches the ground."

The hard part was analyzing what he'd been doing his whole life so he could teach it. For the past three days he'd felt like a centipede tying himself in knots trying to figure out the order his feet moved in.

"Borzhoi, your turn. Everybody listen to him walk."

Teaching these guys to be decent hunters was a pain in the ass. But they were too short on food to wait for them to figure it out on their own.

***

Stitches saw some fan-weed growing by the side of the rhino path. A few cuts with her knife and she dropped the intact plants into her basket. She looked at the accumulation and smiled. Not bad for a half a day's work.

Finding edibles was easier when you spent your time looking instead of gossiping about who'd broken up with whom or what awards the King might give out next. And your basket filled faster when you didn't have to share your finds with the rest of the group.

Gathering on her own worked much better for Stitches than trying to be part of a group. Avoiding the cold shoulders and whispers of 'murderer' was a benefit.

Dumping out a full basket at the commons impressed people. Hungry people didn't carry grudges. They said thank you for food. And they said it louder for filling food like vineroot or eggs.

Which was why Stitches was out here, deeper in the forest than other gatherers had the nerve to go. Everywhere close to camp was picked clean. So she listened to the hunters and went where they'd found game.

Today she was guaranteed a good reception at the common pavilion. A tree had yielded a dozen plum-like fruits. More were still ripening on the tree waiting for her return. Stitches wouldn't be sharing its location with anyone. Or giving the fruit to the Court. They'd all rejected her. It was time to make new friends. Sweets were one way to do that.

Calories were an even better way. She spotted the flowered tendril of a vineroot plant curling around a bush. Her mouth watered. Stitches followed the tendril around to where it poked out of the dirt and started digging with her knife. She'd have to dig down a foot or two, and cut some roots from other plants growing over it to pull this tuber out. Then she'd be done for the day. This would overflow her basket. She'd have to carry the tuber home under her arm.

A rustling made her look up from the work. Figures stood over her. "Um . . . hi?" she essayed.

Then fangs tearing into her flesh made her scream.

***

The stream just downriver from camp was the preferred bathing spot for everyone wanting to avoid cuttlefish. Its cut through the bluff was steep enough to let one person shower in it. The channel on the floodplain was knee-deep at most but some logs and stones had dammed it up to make a pool against the bluff.

It was the ladies' turn to bathe. Ivy stood guard with a pikeaxe, more for cuttlefish than wolves. Only one mollusk had come this far upstream but no one wanted to let another surprise them.

Redinkle and Shellbutton had a surprise of their own for the bathers.

"Who wants to try an experiment?" asked Redinkle, holding up a small crock. She had to almost shout over the sound of the falling water.

"What is it?" said Lady Elderberry.

"Homemade soap. We've been trying different proportions. This one seems to work."

She set the crock on a rock. Scooping out a handful of gray goo, she rubbed it on her face, neck, and farther down. Plunging into the pool rinsed most of it off. She scrubbed at the residue with her hands.

"Oh, my God," said Elderberry. "I've been out of soap for weeks. May I have some?"

"Certainly. We want to know how well it works for everyone."

Shellbutton brought the crock over to her.

Elderberry started with her hair, massaging the goo into her long mop. The excess went onto her face and ears. Then she stood in the waterfall, scrubbing at herself until the soap was gone.

When Elderberry came out from under the waterfall, Mistress Filigree asked, "Is it moisturizing?"

"Hell, no," answered Elderberry. "My skin is wrinkling at the touch of the stuff. It's damn harsh. But I'm clean. God, I feel clean."

Shellbutton poured soap into Filigree's waiting hands.

***

Duke Stonefist burst into his pavilion. "I'm an idiot," he declared.

The padded gambeson he wore under armor was held closed with a dozen pairs of laces. The duke undid half of them before pulling it over his head and dropping it on the floor. A sweat-soaked t-shirt landed on top of the gambeson.

Duchess Roseblossom didn't pause in setting stitches in a ripped jerkin. "What's the matter?"

Stonefist poured some water into a towel and began a hasty spongebath.

"Remember that kid Thistle?"

"The food thief?"

"Yeah. After his second offense I threatened to flog him. Figured that would scare him enough to behave."

She stopped sewing. "It didn't?"

"No. Grabbed some venison and ran into the woods. They caught him when he came back. Court's in an hour." He dropped the towel on the pile. "An hour from when they found me at practice."

"What are you going to do?" asked Roseblossom.

"God. First I'm going to make damn sure he's guilty. Talk to all the witnesses."

"And if he is?"

Stonefist knelt before a wicker chest, pulling out his "Lord High Executioner" outfit. Black linen pants, a white shirt, a black velvet Elizabethan doublet, and matching hat. She let him use getting dressed to delay answering.

"I have to make him stop," said Stonefist. "If he gets away with it more people will start stealing. The ones he's robbed will take food to make up for it. We're too short on food. Everyone's hungry."

Roseblossom didn't say anything.

He sighed. "Too many people know I threatened to flog him. If I don't follow through I destroy my credibility. And then what happens? We have a dozen thieves and mobs lynching them. Anarchy."

The last word was said with the horrified tone of a man describing the worst thing he can imagine.

"So you don't have a choice," said Roseblossom.

"I haven't found an alternative that works yet. Damned well trying to think of one." He pulled black shoes onto his feet. They weren't the proper style for Elizabethan dress. Replacing them had been one of his priorities before . . . this.

Stonefist stood and checked himself with a mirror. He looked every inch a Lord High Executioner. The joke felt less funny today.

He put the mirror down. "If I wasn't such an idiot I would have been coming up with options ever since I made the threat. Or not made it in the first place."

Duchess Roseblossom came up behind him and wrapped her arms around his waist. "You're a good man. You'll find the best option. Even if there isn't a good one."

That produced a sigh. "That's what I'm afraid of. If all I can do is the least bad it's hard to call it justice."

"If there has to be a flogging," she murmured, "Sharpedge could do it."

"No. I'm not going to make my squire do my dirty work. If I pass the sentence I'll carry it out."

He turned around and returned the hug. Then a quick kiss and he was gone.

***

Stonefist pushed himself to get to the court early. Trotting over drove his heart rate up again. He breathed slowly to relax. He'd taken it easy at the fighter practice, critiquing others more than he'd traded blows himself, but his body was still feeling the strain. Not the impression a dignified judge should present. He was hungry, too. Maybe he should have nibbled something from their cache to take the edge off. Didn't want to be too harsh because of low blood sugar. Too late.

King Estoc was already waiting behind the royal pavilion's curtain.

Lord Goldpen, one of the courtiers, slid through the overlap in the curtain. "Your Majesty, Your Grace, everything is in position. The petitioners are waiting."

Estoc nodded. He'd been quiet in his grief.

"Thank you," said Stonefist. His breathing was still faster than he liked. "One minute, please."

"Water for his Grace," snapped Goldpen. Another courtier brought a full mug.

Stonefist took a gulp. Ah, Court water. Not river water boiled and left to settle. Someone had gone all the way to one of the clear streams for this.

Half the mug was enough. He handed it back to the courtier and gave Goldpen a nod.

Lord Goldpen sprang into action. He waved a herald ahead of the monarch. He and a courtier each took hold of the overlapping portions of the curtain. A yank opened it wide enough for king and judge to proceed out side by side.

The herald declared, "The Court of the Lord High Executioner, under the authority of His Majesty King Estoc, is now open. Let those who wish for justice attend."

The king took a couple of steps forward then turned to sit on his throne. It was tucked into a corner, letting him observe but not distract attention from the judge. His presence made the acts of the court official. He didn't participate in the proceedings.

The judge's throne was a fancy chair that Stonefist had acquired to look impressive at feasts. It sat forward of the normal position for the rulers, just within the shadow of the roof. Stonefist sat and gestured to the herald.

"Let House Chevron approach the Lord High Executioner."

Duke Stonefist kept himself from smiling. The herald, at least, wasn't tired of the title.

House Chevron formed a line abreast. The two strongest men held Thistle by the arms in the middle. They were a new house, formed by a merger when the Autocrat forbade cookfires for groups of six or less. Two couples and some strays were now united in pursuit of a firewood ration. The name came from the most common element in the arms of the founders.

Thistle was the youngest of the household. Supposedly eighteen, though Stonefist didn't trust his ID. Clothes and hair were dirtier than those of anyone else in sight. The only bruises on his face were the faded remnant of when he'd resisted after his second offense.

"What is your complaint?" demanded the Lord High Executioner.

Lord Maximus was head of the house. He stepped forward, dragging Thistle with him. He was a fighter, both heavy and rapier, now cutting wood and hauling water. "Theft, Your Grace. This boy grabbed Ivy's meat ration out of hand, ran off, and ate it all. When we found—"

"Let the victim speak."

Maximus closed his mouth.

A woman not much older than Thistle took one step forward and curtsied. "I'm Ivy, your Grace. We were eating around the fire. I was nibbling on some arrowleaves. I eat slow, because the faster I eat the sooner I'm hungry again. Had a bit of venison in my left hand, because, um." She glanced at Thistle. "We've learned not to leave meat on our plate. Well, Thistle stood up and reached past Pritchel and just grabbed it out of my hand. I was so shocked I couldn't say anything until he was around the next tent."

"Thank you. Who witnessed this?" Stonefist raised a hand.

Most of House Chevron raised their hands in response. The judge pointed at the one on the end.

"Um, yer honor, I didn't see him grab the meat, but I saw her holding it and then Thistle ran off and she didn't have it any more."

"Thank you. Next?"

A few offered more details but they all agreed on what happened. Stonefist let them all talk. Someone might have new information. And he wanted time for an idea to pop up.

When the last witness stepped back into line it was clear what had happened. Thistle stared at his feet. Tears dripped off his cheeks.

The judge waved Maximus back. The head of house reluctantly released his grip on the boy, leaving him alone before the throne.

"What do you have to say for yourself, boy?"

"I'm—I'm sorry." Thistle didn't raise his head as he spoke.

"Sorry for what?"

Thistle didn't respond immediately. Stonefist waited.

"For stealing her food, I'm sorry, but I was so hungry!"

The Lord High Executioner said, "We're all hungry."

"I just couldn't help myself, I'm sorry." The boy was looking at the judge now, a desperate expression on his face."

"Well. What punishment would help you help yourself from now on?"

Thistle paled. "I'll—I'll go away. Leave. You won't have to put up with me any more."

Stonefist kept his face in the solemn judge's mask. "Exile is the Kingdom's traditional penalty for most misbehavior. But here and now that's a death sentence."

He raised his voice. "Does anyone think this crime deserves death?"

No one answered. Some of House Chevron shook their heads.

"No exile then. But what will we do with you?"

This would be a perfect moment for the boy to burst out with a solution that would satisfy everyone. Instead he kept crying, eyes on his feet again.

Stonefist sighed. It was time to think of the next boy who'd be tempted to steal. "Thistle, take off your shirt." He turned to his squire, standing in the back corner. "Sharpedge, bring me that rope."

Sharpedge loosened the stay rope from a pole the pavilion didn't need in good weather.

With a wail Thistle dropped to his knees. "Please, I'm sorry, I'll never do it again, I'm sorry!"

The Lord High Executioner took the jute rope. It felt rough and scratchy under his hands. He slid the wood slider down to make it one long loop. "Take off your shirt," he ordered.

Thistle pulled his tunic over his head, leaving him in only modern jockey shorts and leather moccasins. "Please, I'm sorry, I am." He held his hands out as a beggar's.

Inspiration hit.

"Are you sorry?" said Duke Stonefist. "Prove it."

He dropped the rope into Thistle's hands.

That replaced the terror with confusion.

"If you're so sorry, show us. Give yourself the punishment you deserve." Stonefist stood and walked to beside the penitent. A wave of his fingers brought Thistle to his feet.

The watchers, from king to commoners, were silent.

Thistle's jaw worked as he stared at the rope in his hands. He let it slide down until his hands were just above the slider. Then he stood straight, drawing a deep breath. A long moment went by. Shoulders tensed. He flung the rope over his shoulder.

Stonefist could see the flinch on the boy's face as the end of the loop hit his back. The next two blows were softer.

"It's not a punishment if it doesn't hurt, boy," said the Lord High Executioner, his voice pitched for Thistle alone.

The blows became stronger, wilder. The swish of the rope and crack of it meeting flesh drowned out the gasps and mutters from the onlookers. Red welts multiplied across Thistle's back. Blood drops appeared where they met.

A sloppy swing caught Thistle's ear, sending him staggering to the side as he flinched. The next blow drew blood in two places.

"Stop!" cried Ivy. She was crying. When she'd started Stonefist didn't know.

The judge ordered, "Halt."

Thistle bent over, hands on knees, panting. The blood-stained rope dragged in the dirt.

"Lord Maximus," asked Stonefist, "is your household content that justice has been done?"

Hasty nods encouraged the head to say, "Yes, Your Grace."

"Then take him to the Chirurgeon."

Maximus came forward to guide the boy away with a gentle hand on his arm.

Duke Stonefist took his seat again.

"Are there any others seeking justice of the Lord High Executioner?" called the herald.

No one moved. Stonefist had spotted a group in the crowd with the look of a lawsuit. Perhaps they'd changed their mind. Good. People working out their own problems found better results.

"This closes the court of the Lord High Executioner," declared the herald.

Stonefist kept the judge face on. He was still being watched as the crowd dispersed.

"What do you want me to do with this?" asked Sharpedge, picking up the stained rope.

"Put it back on the pole."

"Right there? Where everyone has to look at it?"

Stonefist said, "If they all see it and remember I'm hoping we'll never have to use it again."

***

The House Applesmile pavilion could be divided by a light canvas curtain. Master Sweetbread and Mistress Tightseam would put it up when they wanted some privacy from the younger members of the household.

Now Mistress Tightseam was sacrificing the curtain. Shellbutton's fondness for light linen dresses hadn't served her well in the disaster. Between kneeling in the dirt to gather plants and being washed on river rocks, they were tattered beyond patching. New clothes were needed. The curtain was the best fabric available.

Producing a dress was no test of Mistress Tightseam's skill. The hard part was wasting as little fabric as possible. A few members of the Kingdom were spinning yarn from local plant fibers, but they were a long way from making enough for cloth. Fortunately she remembered some historic outfits designed more for thrifty production than a flattering appearance.

Thus when Lord Goldpen arrived at House Applesmile he saw Shellbutton lying contorted on the curtain as Redinkle marked where to cut with a bit of charcoal. This discomposed the voluble courtier enough he stood there in silence.

Mistress Tightseam eyed him warily. Goldpen was one of the late Queen Camellia's favorites. No one wanted to punish him for his support of her, but Autocrat Sharpquill did stick him with delivering bad news.

"May I help you, my lord?" prompted Tightseam.

Goldpen started. "Oh, yes. We're doing a roll call." He checked his slate. "There are eight in your household, yes? Have you seen them all today?"

"We were all here at breakfast. Right?" Tightseam looked to her daughter.

Redinkle nodded. "Newman's hunting, Goldenrod's gathering, and the boys are at the charcoal pit. I don't remember where Dad went."

"He's cooking at the common pavilion," supplied Shellbutton.

"That's all of us," said Mistress Tightseam. "Why do you ask?"

Goldpen flinched. He carefully put a checkmark on his slate. "Um. A hunting party found a skeleton this morning."

"A skeleton? Whoever it is must've been missing for a while."

"Not decayed, Mistress. Eaten."

Shellbutton said, "Ewww."

"I must ask. Have any of you seen La—I mean, have you seen Stitches today?"

"I haven't. Girls?"

The younger women shook their heads.

"Thank you. I'm sorry to trouble you."

The courtier went into the lane and stood a moment studying his slate. Then he looked around, studying the people walking about and checking the slate again. His eyes locked on a woman in a dark brown dress and he strode down the lane toward her. "Lady Belladonna!"

Redinkle said, "They must be making him talk to everybody if he's asking her about the roll call."

Belladonna turned to look at the courtier, met his eyes with no change in her expression, then turned away. He caught up and tugged at her sleeve. They couldn't hear what he said, but Belladonna stopped and listened to him.

"Is she pregnant?" asked Shellbutton.

"No way," replied Redinkle. "No guy would put up with her long enough."

Shellbutton looked hard. "That's a distinct belly bulge."

Mistress Tightseam turned to look. "Belly's bulging but her tits are shrinking. Not pregnant. I'd bet she's hiding a vineroot under her dress so she doesn't have to share. Back in position, girl. Gossiping won't get you a new dress."

***

Autocrat Sharpquill looked up from his laptop. "Good evening, Your Majesty."

Everyone in the pavilion hastily stood.

"Good evening. May I have a moment of your time?" said King Estoc.

"I am at Your Majesty's disposal." That might not be an expression given the look on the king's face.

Estoc took a seat across the table from Sharpquill. He made a shooing gesture, sending the staffers out.

The Autocrat sat back down. Lady Cinnamon slid onto the bench beside him, her thigh against his. He felt strength flow into him from the connection. If the king wanted her to leave he'd have to ask, and give a reason, Sharpquill decided.

Her presence didn't seem to bother the king. Something else did. He wasn't eager to bring it up.

Master Sharpquill broke the silence. "Thank you for supporting the theft trial this afternoon, Your Majesty."

King Estoc leaned forward. "You're welcome. My authority was used to force a teenage boy to beat himself bloody. I'm glad you're happy about it."

"Duke Stonefist has taken on a difficult job. There's no easy answers when we have people taking food from each other's mouths."

"Fine. It's his job. Well, I'm here to tell you my job is expiring. There's three weeks left in the reign. Then I'm going to go cut down trees and chase deer and someone else can take responsibility for all this horrible shit."

Sharpquill's shoulders hunched up. His neck tensed. He clamped his jaws shut to keep his initial response from escaping.

Cinnamon spoke first, her voice gentle. "Your Majesty, we need you." Her hand slid up Sharpquill's back, stroking, trying to soothe him, and failing.

"You need someone. It doesn't have to be me," snarled the king.

He'd found diplomatic words now. "Your Majesty, we don't have the time to spare for a tournament. We're too close to the edge. It would mean people missing days of meals. And if they're too weak to hunt or gather we won't be able to catch back up."

"Bullshit. Just say, 'We're having a tourney today.' Line them up. We'll be done in a few hours."

Master Sharpquill leaned into Cinnamon. He drew calm from her. "That's fine for those few who've been practicing their skills. For everyone who put down their tourney weapon to do the work that's been keeping us alive. . ." His voice grew harsher on the last phrase. "They would be excluded from any chance of winning. What would that do to morale? And to the legitimacy of the winner?"

That made the king think a moment. "Okay. There's three weeks left in the reign. That's time to prepare. We can have tourney and coronation the same day."

"For each contender, we'd lose three weeks of their work. Plus the work of the artisans repairing armor and consorts and friends cheering them on. We can't spare that."

Frustration was clear on Estoc's face. "How many contenders do you think there'll be?"

Lady Cinnamon's grip on his arm kept the Autocrat in his seat. He said, "Your Majesty," in a tone which made it a euphemism for 'you idiot.' "This is not a contest for a ceremonial position in a hobby group. This is the most powerful office in a life-or-death situation. Who wins that tourney will decide who lives or dies here. Everyone will show up. Some will be there just to keep someone else from winning. And everyone will be there to watch."

Estoc laughed. "Most powerful? Then why am I asking you to escape from it?"

"Because you can fire me. Please do. You know exactly how relieved I'd be."

Lady Cinnamon said, "Gentlemen. Please. This is being too heated. Let's take a moment for some slow deep breaths."

Neither man did the breathing exercise. They did stay silent and wait for their adrenaline levels to recede.

King Estoc said quietly, "I'm not supposed to do this forever."

"It's not forever. We're in a tight spot because we've used up the closest food sources. There's more out there for us to find. When we have enough for a surplus to give people two days off a week we'll schedule the tourney. And we can have the coronation the same day. Is that acceptable, Your Majesty?"

"I guess." Estoc waved his hands then dropped them to the table. Even more softly he said, "I'm not supposed to do this alone." He started to cry.

Autocrat Sharpquill felt ashamed. The man had watched his wife killed before his eyes a month ago.

Cinnamon went around the table and hugged Estoc. Sharpquill followed and put a hand on his monarch's shoulder. It heaved with sobs.

***

"The birds are quiet," said Newman.

"So?" replied Bodkin.

"There's probably a predator about. Keep your eyes open."

The six hunters drifted into a horseshoe formation as the flankers kept looking behind themselves. The woods were dense enough that something fifty yards away might only be seen for a moment.

They didn't need to look that hard. When they came upon a clearing the predators were on the far side of it.

"Holy shit! Orcs!" cried Deadeye.

"Calm down," said Bodkin. "We don't know anything about them. Ugly doesn't mean they're evil."

Newman studied the strangers. They were humanoid but not human. Their heights were all in the normal human range but the shoulders were wider than a gorilla's. Thick arm muscles flexed as they leveled wood spears at the hunters. Some carried two or three spears. The tips were bare wood scraped to points. As the strangers hooted and grunted at each other their lips drew back to reveal shark-like triangular teeth and pointed tusks.

Newman heard the other hunters muttering. The green skin and lack of hair or clothes bothered them more than evidence the strangers were pure carnivores.

"We know they're all male," he said.

"So probably a hunting party," said Bodkin.

"Yeah. That's who's been leaving those piles of deer bones around."

The humanoids were discussing the hunting party, with lots of yells and pointing. *Shocked to see a new species in the woods, or just naturally loud talkers?* wondered Newman.

"We should report this," said Leadsmith, edging back into the woods.

Deadeye snapped, "We can't lead them back to the camp."

"Let's see if they want to talk," said Bodkin. "If we can trade with them we'll be better off."

"Trade what?" said Deadeye.

"Tools," said Newman. "They don't even have stone spearheads. They'd probably swap a ton of food for metal points."

The discussion on the far side ended with all of the strangers turning to face the hunters. The tallest of them yelled something. Five spears flew across the clearing.

"Shit! Down!" Newman drew an arrow from his quiver before going flat on the ground. The rest dropped too except for Deadeye. He hopped left and right, dodging the spears.

A couple flew close by him. The others stuck in the ground behind the hunters.

Newman rose to a kneeling stance with an arrow already nocked. He sent it into the chest of the tall one then dropped as more spears flew. As soon as they hit he put a second arrow a few inches from the first.

The tallest stranger tugged at one of the arrows sticking in his chest, snarled, then waved his companions into the woods ahead of him. Their complexion quickly blended with the leaves.

"Anyone hurt?" asked Bodkin.

"Got my arm," gasped Leadsmith.

Newman stood sentry while the rest performed first aid. He kept watch behind the whole way back to camp.

***

Newman and Deadeye went to the Autocrat to report the encounter. He cut them off and dispatched a runner. "Wait until the Knight Marshal, Count Dirk, gets here. He's in charge of fighting."

A minute later Dirk arrived, asking, "What's up?" The count had come from weapons practice. He still wore most of his armor. Sweat stained the thick cloth underneath.

"Contact with hostile locals," said Newman.

Dirk snapped from relaxed and tired to laser-focused. "What kind? Civilized?"

Newman stood straighter. "No, sir. No clothes, no metal or stone tools."

"But you think they're intelligent?"

"They used wooden spears, no stone points, and spoke to each other before attacking us."

"Casualties?"

"One wounded on each side."

Dirk sat on the Autocrat's table. The edge of his leg armor cut a notch in the smooth wood. "Okay, give me the whole story. From first sighting."

Deadeye interpolated colorful details into Newman's dry report.

"Green skin, tusks, broad muscular shoulders . . . are we talking orcs?" asked Count Dirk.

"Totally orcs," said Deadeye.

"Of course. We have dragons, so of course there's orcs."

Autocrat Sharpquill asked, "Are we at war, then?"

Dirk shook his head. "No. Young hot-heads attacking a rival hunting party isn't war. We need to find their home village and talk to the elders. Demarcate hunting territories, maybe do some trade."

He thought a moment longer. "For now, I'll attach a fighter to each hunting party for security. We'll send out patrols to look for the village. And make sure the gate guards are taking the job seriously."

"I presume you want your fighters released from hauling wood and water and shit?" asked the Autocrat.

"No, it's good exercise for them," said Dirk with a grin. "But you'll have to schedule around their patrols."

"Just give me twelve hours' notice." The Autocrat turned to his laptop to check the spreadsheet for workers.

Count Dirk waved the hunters ahead of him as they left. "Newman, you don't seem very bothered by finding monsters here."

"I guess I'm more comfortable with strangers trying to kill me in the wild than dealing with protocol for nobility. Your excellency."

***

The fish was delicious. Even with no spices to work with Master Sweetbread had crisped the pink flesh to add a contrast to the base taste.

"Where'd you find this?" asked Pernach. He still had soot on his face. He and Pinecone had skipped bathing when they smelled dinner cooking.

Newman finished chewing his bite. Just having some protein that wasn't venison would make this a good meal. Sweetbread made it something to savor. "It found me. Lord Badelaire grabbed me after the hunting allocation and offered a trade."

"How'd he catch them?" Shellbutton wiped up some juice with a bit of vineroot.

Mistress Tightseam answered, "He has a rod and reel. I've seen him on the riverbank."

"Yes, he's out there every day," confirmed Goldenrod.

Sweetbread slid the last bit of fish onto a plate. He put the frying pan aside to cool and sat down with his family. "Pity he can't bring in more. This probably has nutrients we're not getting elsewhere."

"We should make some nets. That would catch more." Goldenrod looked at the piece of fish on her fork, counting to ten before eating.

Pinecone laughed. "Who are you going to kill to get the rope? Cuirass and Pliers broke each other's noses over a twenty foot piece."

"What about the stuff you made from tree bark?"

"Master Chisel's replaced most of it," said Sweetbread. "It stretches in the rain."

"Hmmm."

Pernach shared the tale of someone who'd tried to make rope but had been sent back to food gathering by the Autocrat after four failed attempts.

"Weirs!"

The rest of the table looked at each other to check if anyone understood Goldenrod's outburst.

Newman felt obliged to provide a straight line. "What?"

"Fishing weirs. They're like a dam that catches fish." She looked around and found no support. "They're good at catching fish. It was in the Magna Carta. The Barons made King John tear down his weirs. Cost him a lot of revenue."

"We can't dam that river. It's too big," said Sweetbread.

"We don't need to. Imagine . . . oh, a basket in the river. Water goes through, minnows go through, eating fish get caught."

"So a wicker-work dam," said Tightseam.

"Yes."

Pernach chuckled. "The cuttlefish will love that. They'll eat half the construction crew."

"The cuttlefish haven't killed anyone yet," snapped Goldenrod. Though like most people she'd switched from bathing in the river to a stream.

Diplomacy was called for. Newman said, "We'd just need some spearmen guarding the builders."

"You'd think they'd have learned to avoid us by now," said Pinecone.

Sweetbread shrugged. "The six foot long ones are just as stupid as the six inch ones at home."

"Yeah, but octopi are smart. They should be smart as an octopus."

"Wait until we get to the ocean. Imagine smart octopi the size of a football field." Newman grinned at the shivers he caused.

Goldenrod didn't shiver. She was thinking.

***

Soap making used ordinary kitchen pots and a cookfire. Redinkle and Shellbutton did their work in House Applesmile's kitchen, maneuvering around the meal schedule.

That made it easy for Autocrat Sharpquill to find them.

They started at his, "Good morning, ladies."

Redinkle's stomach twisted when she saw the look on his face. "Good day, my lord."

Shellbutton just offered a nervous curtsy.

"I've heard about your work," said the Autocrat. "I admire your ingenuity. You'll both receive crafting awards when we have the leisure for such things."

His pause seemed to demand a response.

Redinkle offered, "Thank you, my lord."

"Yes. It's very clever. But we can't eat it. Can't drink it. And the lard you're using could have gone into meals. We need those calories. We need your labor producing food, not soap. I formally order you to stop making soap and return to productive labor. You'll be assigned duties if you can't find any."

"Just throw this away?" Redinkle gestured at the steaming pots.

The Autocrat relented. "You may finish this batch. But no more. Understood?"

"Yes, my lord."

Once he was gone Shellbutton demanded, "Why did you let him push us around like that? We should fight back."

"We will." Redinkle smiled. "We'll get help."

When the finished batch was decanted into another crock the two women took it to the Chiurgeon's tent.

"Lady Burnout, we have the soap you wanted."

"Good. This should last me about a week."

"We can't make you any more. Master Sharpquill ordered us to stop."

"He what?"

When that was explained Redinkle and Shellbutton went to the silver smith's shop.

"Mistress Filigree? We won't be able to deliver that soap to you."

The next stop was an elaborate pavilion next to the Royal one.

"Duchess Roseblossom, we most humbly apologize . . ."

***

"Newman! Hey, Newman!"

The sound of someone crashing through branches was almost louder than the shouts.

Newman called, "Over here!"

Bodkin stumbled through the trees. He'd been running hard. Sweat stained his shirt's chest down to the belly button. "Something grabbed (pant) Crowfeather. (pant) You've got to (pant) help find him."

"Grabbed? By what? Orcs?"

"Dunno. Just heard him yell."

"Right." Newman whistled his team back to him. "Let's go."

It was almost a mile to the site. A couple of Newman's men fell behind. He just told them not to let themselves be snatched next and followed Bodkin.

"Here." Bodkin pointed to several hunters standing around. Then he bent over and vomited, panting with exhaustion.

"What happened?" said Newman.

"Dunno." The guy in the striped tunic was looking in every direction at once and standing close to his buddies. "I mean, he yelled for help. When we got here we heard him being dragged away."

So much for getting a useful briefing.

"Fine. We're going after him." Newman raised his voice. "This could be an attempt to lure us into an ambush. We need to watch for anything waiting for us. Deadeye, Borzhoi, watch up in the trees. Husky, Beargut, check for stuff hiding in the bushes. Sing out if there's anything suspicious. I'm going to be head down following the trail. Move out."

The trail wasn't hard to follow. Crowfeather had dragged his feet, making lines in the leaves and mold. Two orcs were pulling him along. The bare feet had four toes and a more squared-off heel than human feet.

Newman kept at a trot. The other hunters mostly straggled behind him. Crashing noises said a few were keeping up to his sides, forcing their way through dense growth the orcs had avoided.

After half a mile the trail went sideways for a few yards. Crowfeather must have tried to get away. Drying red blood stained a tree trunk. Only orc footprints led away, but one set was deeper. The human was being carried.

More red blood had dripped to the left of the footprints. Newman pressed on, ignoring the alarmed conversation behind him.

The blood kept spotting the forest floor. A scratch should have clotted quickly. Newman hoped it was just a scalp wound, not something more severe.

The same orc was still carrying Crowfeather when the trail reached the bank of North Creek, a mile from the escape attempt. Newman waded across carefully. It was full of stones that could break an ankle or just tip him into the water.

The far bank had no tracks, only some depressions that might be old orc footprints washed by rain.

Newman looked at the men lining the other bank. "Deadeye, go downstream a hundred yards and look for tracks. Bring two men to guard you. You and you, come with me."

Wading a hundred yards upstream through the cold water left Newman's feet numb. He found no trace of Crowfeather or his captors. He recrossed and walked to where they'd emerged from the woods.

Deadeye was waiting with the others. "Find anything?" he asked. "I struck out."

Newman shook his head. "Then we've lost him."

"You can't give up!" said Striped-shirt.

"We don't know where to look."

"So we split up!"

Newman looked around. "There's eight of us here. More of us are straggling through the woods or stopped to catch their breath. We're already so split up we could have lost someone else to the orcs and not know it. We can't spread out more."

"He's my friend! I'm not going to stop. I'll go find him myself." Striped-shirt was almost incoherent with anger.

"No."

"How are you going to stop me?"

Newman's voice was calm. "I'll break your nose, knock you down, and stomp on you until you have better sense." He raised his voice to address the whole group, including a couple just straggling out of the woods. "There aren't enough of us to trade warm bodies for cold ones. Everyone back at camp needs us for food and protection. We can't wander off and be picked off one at a time."

No one answered him. Striped-shirt's mouth worked but he didn't say anything.

"Let's head back and collect the stragglers. Remember who you were hunting with. We need to check if anyone else is missing."

***

Newman found himself drafted to add his prestige as a hunter to Goldenrod's effort to recruit weir builders.

Master Chisel came down to the river bank with them. "I can't put much effort into this. We need a storm shelter. The tents are standing up to the rain we've had so far, but if we get one with strong winds . . ."

"I just need your help with the posts," said Goldenrod. "Once those are in filling in the rest can be unskilled labor."

She sketched her design in the mud of the bank. Newman kept his spear ready. Some cuttlefish would wrap a tentacle around an ankle to pull someone into the river.

"Every two feet?" blurted Chisel.

"Doing the basket weave needs them close together."

"You need verticals close together, but they don't all need to be braced. Seven posts, every four feet."

Goldenrod opened her mouth, closed it, then said, "Thank you," with her best smile.

***

Breakfast for House Applesmile was eggs of the local bird-equivalents. They were edible, and probably nutritious, but there were no requests for seconds. Shellbutton waved about a bowl of leftovers. The only suggestion was to take it to the common pavilion.

Master Sweetbread looked up at approaching footsteps. "Good morning, my Lord Autocrat."

The rest of the table repeated the greeting.

Autocrat Sharpquill nodded in reply. He focused on the two youngest women. "You two. Get back to work on the damn soap."

"Yes, my lord," answered Redinkle. She was careful not to smile.

He turned on his heel and stalked off.

"That was quicker than I expected," said Mistress Tightseam.

Redinkle shrugged. "We spread the word to the well-connected."

Goldenrod leaned toward Newman. "See? They may not be written down, but our government does have checks and balances."

***

"I'm amazed you don't have heat stroke in that junk," muttered a hunter.

Strongarm laughed. "Sometimes we do. But it happens in sunlight. These woods are nicely shady."

The trees were dense enough to give cover to orcs as well as deer, which is why Strongarm was accompanying the trio of bowmen. Lone orcs had wounded hunters before. To their relief he'd covered the edges of his armor with strips of cloth or leather so he wouldn't jingle-jangle all the game away.

Not that he'd gotten to fight an orc yet. Usually his contribution was to help carry the dead deer.

The hunters did appreciate that.

Today the deer were more skittish than usual. They'd seen glimpses of some bucks, but they were running. None stayed in sight long enough for an arrow shot.

Strongarm focused on moving quietly. The sooner they caught some meat, the sooner he could be inside the walls taking his armor off.

They were headed for a thinner patch of forest. Maybe they'd get some shots in there.

A hunter gasped. Strongarm looked up. A band of orcs faced them thirty yards away. Ten—no, twelve of them. Too many to fight.

"Run," ordered Strongarm. "I'll hold them off. Run!"

He charged the orcs, finally being the hero he'd always wanted to be. Arrows hissed past him as the hunters each loosed before fleeing.

His shield brushed aside the lead orc's spear. He swung his sword into the side of its head. The wooden weapon had been made lethal by lining each side of it with nails filed to sharp points. A few nails stayed in the orc's skull as Strongarm pulled his sword away.

A step and a twist of his hips put Strongarm's full strength into a backhand blow at the next orc. This time he aimed for the neck. The nails tore through orcflesh in a spray of orange blood.

The third orc thrust a spear at his head. The shield deflected it. The orc dropped his weapon to grab the shield.

His sword parried another spear. The orc kept pressing, binding the weapons together.

Strongarm took a step back to keep his balance. More orcs came up. One grabbed his leg. He landed on his back with a grunt.

The crash freed his sword. He couldn't swing it but managed to smash a nose with the hilt.

A voice barked commanding syllables. Every orc grabbed a limb. One sat on his chest.

Straining couldn't break their grip. "Apples, dammit, my safeword is apples!"

The shield and sword were dragged away. Orcs poked at the armor, pinching the flesh underneath as they found gaps. Claws cut straps and tore at his clothing.

Strongarm realized he wasn't going to be speared through the eyeslit of his helmet. "So it's to be torture. I can cope with torture."

The leg armor and codpiece were pulled off first. They weren't bothering with the helmet or breastplate. He contemplated being eaten alive feet first. "Well, I'll bleed out before it gets too bad."

A chill breeze hit him as his pants and underwear were ripped away. "Yeah, look at that dick, boys. Jealous, aren't you?"

The barking voice issued another command. The orcs flipped him onto his belly. The changing grips gave Strongarm a chance to kick one hard enough to produce a grunt. Then he was immobilized again.

Claws tore at straps and clothes again. His kidney belt was pulled free. Soon his hips were exposed to air again.

The orc sitting on his shoulders got off. He used the freedom to try to pull his arms loose without success.

The biggest orc put his hands on Strongarm's back and his legs against the man's.

Strongarm said, "Oh, no. You are not—"

He screamed.

***

Chisel's apprentices were shaping tree trunks into pointed posts. To Goldenrod they looked like sharpened pencils. The points were driven into the riverbed by hitting the eraser end with sledge hammers.

A sledge-wielder yelped as his feet went out from under him. His partner grabbed an arm, pulling to keep his head above water.

Three royal guards gathered around plunging their spears into the water. One yelled, "Hah!" and levered his spear up.

The cuttlefish impaled on it waved every purple tentacle, trying to find its attacker. Another guard grabbed the spear to heave the beast onto the bank.

The third guard drove a spear through it, pinning it to the ground. Other spearmen stabbed it until it lay still.

"I wish these were edible," said one. "Must be fifty pounds of meat on it." Another mimed retching.

Tapping sounded again. The carpenters had found their sledges and gone back to work.

The Autocrat had come to check on the progress. "This had better work," he said to Goldenrod. "You've diverted a lot of labor to this little project."

"We need the fish, my lord. It's good protein."

"I'm not worried about the nutritional value of the fish. Just whether this thing will catch any of them. And if it will last long enough to be worthwhile."

Goldenrod had evaded the Autocrat's process for allocating labor to projects. The Court was hesitant to authorize new ideas. But it seemed receiving forgiveness in lieu of permission would have to wait on delivering fish.

***

"We found him! He got free, he was halfway back home. He's in bad shape though."

Lady Burnout ignored the brash fighters escorting Strongarm into her tent. She focused on the injured man, assessing his injuries. His halting walk indicated more damage than was visible on the surface.

"Help him up on the table," she ordered.

Strongarm lay on his side, tugging on the borrowed tabard to cover himself.

"Good. Off with you, boys, go kick some ass," said Lady Burnout.

The fighters clattered out with promises of vengeance. Strongarm didn't answer them.

"I'm going to start by disinfecting those claw marks. This will sting."

"'Sokay." He didn't look at her.

None of the scratches were deep enough to be dangerous. Bruising was extensive.

He flipped to his other side without protest.

That side was no different.

"We need to talk about the elephant in the room," she said.

Strongarm hunched his shoulders.

"Look . . . back at my old emergency room we had a patient. Nasty guy. Gangbanger, killed three rivals in drive-bys. One day he got drunk off his home turf and another gang grabbed him. Took him to their clubhouse, raped him for hours, then dropped him on a playground. He came in the ER walking the way you did just now."

Strongarm took a few deep breaths. "Does anyone else know?"

"Some might guess." She'd cleaned some orange streaks off his thighs.

"Shit."

"I need to examine and treat you."

"I know. Just . . . I don't want to be on my belly."

"Can you lift up your knee?"

That gave her access enough. The tears were scabbing over. She applied ointment and, after dithering, the last dose of injectable antibiotic. He didn't complain.

After washing her hands Lady Burnout walked around to talk face to face. "How are you feeling?"

"Like hell."

"I figured that. What else?"

Strongarm stayed silent. Burnout bit her tongue and out-waited him.

"Why?" he burst out. "They're not human, I'm not one of them. Why would they even be interested in doing that to me?"

"Humans fuck other species. How many sheep jokes have you heard?"

"Oh, I'm a sheep. Now I know what they'll call me."

"You're a good fighter. What did you do to the orcs before you went down?"

"Killed two." He'd seen the bodies when he woke. "Might've hurt some more."

"So they'd be mad. Might have wanted revenge like those gangbangers. Or, yeah, it could be the sheep thing. We've never seen one of their females."

Strongarm was looking past the wall of the tent. "I thought I was dead when I fell down. I was just glad I'd gotten more of them than they were killing in me."

"We'll get you back in shape and you can up that score some more."

***

"What the hell?" said Newman as they came around the bend in the rhino trail.

A pit had been dug in the trail. Dirt covered the bushes on both sides of the trail. The depression was cone shaped, at least six or eight feet down at the deepest point.

All the Wolfheads laughed. "You didn't hear about that?" asked Husky.

"No," said Beargut. "Going to share?"

Borzhoi told the story. "The royal guard has to work now. They decided to justify their existence by bringing in some big game. So they came up with a plan to trap a rhino in a pit."

Footprints of the massive herbivores were visible in the dirt.

"How'd that work out for them?" asked Newman.

"They'd gotten this far when a herd, I mean crash, came down. The bull didn't even slow down. The cows were fine. The first calf struggled but made it out. The second calf was stuck. Kept trying to get over the edge, couldn't." Borzhoi took a sip from his canteen.

"Well?" demanded Beargut.

"Then the cow at the end of the crash put her horns under the little guy's butt. He flew out, at least three feet off the ground. The royal guard stopped wanting to hunt rhinos."

***

Today was Strongarm's first patrol since it happened two weeks ago. There were more patrols than hunting parties now. Autocrat Sharpquill wanted the orcs cleared away, even if doing it frightened the game.

Armoring up wasn't new. Strongarm had been training new fighters since he'd healed enough to walk smoothly. He hadn't volunteered for any patrols but Captain Spear needed another experienced fighter for this one.

When Spear asked if he was up for it Strongarm answered "of course" as if he'd been waiting to be asked.

Whether he was actually up for it . . . he wanted to know.

The newbies on the patrol wore the usual mix of borrowed and improvised armor. Strongarm inspected them. The few problems were fixed with duct tape or leather cords. A couple newbies were missing gorgets. They'd just have to hope no orc hit them in the throat.

Crusher was the patrol leader. He ordered the other veteran, Maximus, to take point. "Strongarm, you're in the middle with me." The newbies formed a single file before and after them. They marched out the gate.

The cleared zone outside the walls was a little wider. The sun beat down on his helmet, starting a bit of sweat. Some women were out with blades, hacking at any bush that might offer cover to an enemy.

Strongarm could hear the usual forest noises as they walked up to the trees. Wind in the leaves. Birds complaining at each other. Nothing indicating a large animal.

He scanned the trees, checking for anything behind them. Just more trees. He saw an arm in the corner of his eye but when he snapped his head to look it was just a branch.

He followed Crusher past the first tree. There wasn't anything behind it. He looked left to right to check for orcs. Nothing. At the second tree he stopped. The newbies behind him pulled up to not bump into him.

Crusher kept moving deeper into the woods.

Strongarm tried to follow him. His feet wouldn't move. He looked down. Willed the right foot to take a step. Nothing. Looked up and around to see if something had snuck up while he stared at his feet.

He heard Crusher order a halt then walk back. "Hey. It's just a walk in the woods. Last two times we didn't see anything."

"Yeah, I know. I just . . ." Maybe if he picked up a foot and put it back down again? No, that wasn't happening either.

Behind him a newbie muttered, "What's going on?" Another shushed him.

Talking himself into moving wasn't working. Nor did ordering himself. Now he was fretting about the anxiety he was feeling over having an anxiety attack. Bad feedback loop.

Crusher said quietly, "Okay, not today then. Go to the gate, ask one of the guards to switch places with you. Go."

Strongarm turned around and walked briskly back.

Behind him Crusher snarled, "Shut the fuck up, Rivet. He's killed orcs. I've seen the bodies. You haven't."

***

Lady Burnout held up the tent flap as Constable and another man carried Belladonna in. "What's the trouble?"

"She screamed, grabbed her belly, and passed out," grunted Constable. "I'd guess the baby's coming."

"I hope not. She's six months along at most." Burnout hadn't noticed any sign of pregnancy when doing the rape exam almost four months ago. Belladonna had avoided the chiurgeon since, but camp gossip had passed word of her swollen belly.

"Looks overdue to me," said Constable

Apprentice Elderberry helped him lay her on the exam table. Lying flat showed her belly's true size.

"Damn. My wife didn't get that big with either of hers," said the other man.

"Give me room, please." They stepped out of Lady Burnout's way as she pulled up Belladonna's dress. The pregnant belly stretched as the baby kicked and pushed. "Not having a contraction." She paused. "That looks . . . wrong somehow."

She turned her attention to the patient's vitals. Pulse weak and fast. Skin very pale. Fingernails stayed white when pressed. If she had internal bleeding there wasn't much chance of saving her. Checking the underwear showed no blood stains so not a miscarriage. Yet.

"I'm going to have to wake her up so I can talk to her. Hand me the smelling salts."

Elderberry held the vial out to the chiurgeon, who waved it under the unconscious woman's nose.

Belladonna opened her eyes and screamed.

Lady Burnout grabbed her shoulders and tried to calm her. The patient just turned away, still screaming. Burnout kept talking until something wet splashed her arm. She turned to look at the swollen belly.

A black claw poked out just below the sternum. Blood sprayed from the hole. The claw sliced through skin to the belly button, letting more blood flow.

Belladonna choked and went silent.

A green-skinned head poked out of the slit. A wide grin displayed dozens of shark teeth.

The creature sprang free of Belladonna's body like a carnivorous frog. It slid underneath the tent wall and vanished.

"Get it! Kill it!" cried Constable. He led the other man out of the tent at a sprint.

Elderberry had her finger on Belladonna's neck. "No pulse," she said.

"Damn. Start compressions," said Burnout.

As the apprentice started CPR the doctor opened up the wound to check how bad the bleeding was. Then she stepped back. "Never mind. She's gone."

When the men returned Burnout was making notes on the extent of the damage.

"Goddamned thing was faster than a cat," reported Constable. "It went over the fence into the woods. What the hell happened here?"

Burnout pulled open the collapsed belly skin. "Clearly some kind of parasite was growing inside her. It must have been feeding on her internally. There's whole organs missing. Womb and ovaries. Most of the small intestine. Half the liver. One kidney."

She wiped her hands. "There isn't nearly as much blood as there should be for this damage. It must have spread a coagulant. All the blood is from the skin cuts."

"What was it?" he asked. "Where did it come from?"

"I don't know. I don't know."

***

The hard part of weaving the weir was finding enough long pieces of wood. Long branches from cut trees and scraps from shaping logs were the best she could do.

Goldenrod's personal charisma wasn't enough to overcome Autocrat Sharpquill's frown. She had to finish the weir by herself. Once she had a stack of cross-pieces by the weir it was time to find some spearmen.

Goldenrod suspected the eagerness of the volunteers wasn't for the chance to kill some cuttlefish. She didn't want to subject her bras to river water so she did the work in just shorts and a t-shirt. This made the guards very attentive to her.

She'd rather they were watching out to see the cuttlefish approaching. None of them had dragged her under the water but more days than not she wound up clinging to the weir while the spearmen stabbed an annoying critter.

They did seem to be getting scarcer.

Actually building the weir wasn't hard, just tedious. She wove a cross-piece back and forth between the poles sticking out of the water. Once it held in place she shoved it to the bottom.

The shoreward side of the V was done. Working in the deeper water left Goldenrod immersed to her neck. The guards didn't mind since she had to wade back for the next piece of wood each time.

Her legs stung where they'd been jabbed by the rough ends of cross-pieces sticking into the hinge of the V. She'd have to trim those later but she wanted to finish the sides first. The weir was working. She saw fish bump against the finished shoreward side until they found their way through the gap of the hinge.

***

Strongarm waited until all the other patients had left before approaching the chiurgeon's tent. "Milady?"

"Enter!" ordered Lady Burnout. "Oh, hello, Strongarm. What can I do for you today?" She waved toward the small table with chairs and tea cups, inviting him to sit down for another chat.

"Um . . . my stomach's bothering me."

"Onto the table, then."

He lay down and pulled his shirt up to his sternum.

"Symptoms?"

"Diarrhea. And . . . well . . . it feels like something's moving in there." He traced a circle below his belly button.

Burnout laid her hands flat on the indicated area. Pressed down. Waited. Shifted her hands. "There is something in there." A breath. "Maybe more than one."

"Oh, God. I was hoping you'd tell me it was gas."

"There's a parasite. Parasites are treatable. We may have to try a few different things."

"Okay. Um . . . I heard about what happened to Belladonna."

"Everybody did."

"Do you know where her . . . thing came from?"

"No." She decided a dead patient's confidentiality mattered less than a live one's need to know. "She was raped on the night we arrived here. Wouldn't say who did it. All I could tell was that it was more than one attacker."

"Shit. She could have been caught by orcs."

"Maybe. Ah!" Lady Burnout began digging through storage boxes tucked under her examining table. "I took a swab of her for DNA evidence, because I hadn't noticed we'd gone anywhere. Completely forgot about it with all the excitement. Here it is." She dropped a ziplock on the bench.

"And I took a swab of you. Because habit is powerful. Ha!" She stood up and grabbed the first one. "Now we compare."

Strongarm sat up to watch. The two swabs had dried to almost identical orange-brown blobs. "Fuck."

"Well." Lady Burnout felt this was a time to say something comforting. But she couldn't think of a thing to say.

"Belladonna was raped by orcs," said Strongarm. "Is that how she was infected by that . . . whatever it was?"

Unable to find another answer, Burnout admitted, "It could be. All we know for sure was you were both attacked and the attackers had the same color . . . fluid."

"And we have parasites."

"You have a few small parasites. She had one big one. So that's an argument it's something different. I assumed it was a venereal infection originally. Could still be one, just parasitic rather than bacterial."

"Shit. Orc clap." Strongarm brooded. "I'm infected, whatever it is. How dangerous is it? Could it kill me?"

"I don't know. Most parasites try to avoid killing their hosts. There's ways to get rid of them." She pulled out the emergency whiskey bottle hidden under the exam table. She considered cup sizes and just handed him the bottle.

Strongarm took a swig. "Will this kill them?"

"Not directly. It's absorbed too soon. But if we get your blood alcohol level high enough it might get them. Let's call this experiment one. Keep drinking."

She wrote in her notebook. Every so often she prompted him to take another slug of whiskey.

"Crap." Burnout put down her pen. "The hunters find worms in some of the deer they catch. I told them to burn the infected ones. Didn't ask for samples. Maybe I should have."

"Yeah, it'd be nice to know what the hell's happening to me."

"I'll do research. And I'll let you know what I find out."

"Thanks."

***

Goldenrod's original plan for holding the fish failed. The borrowed baskets tore loose from the weir or let the fish escape as she levered the baskets clear of the weir.

The fourth experiment was half a dozen net laundry bags nailed to a wooden frame. When she went back to check on it the guards had to spear a cuttlefish with its tentacles buried in the bottom bag.

The other bags were full of fish.

Goldenrod managed to get the frame to shore on her own. She needed both guards to help her haul it out of the water. Whippet and Husky were on water hauling duty. They earned a fish each helping on the steep path up the bluff.

Master Chisel's shop was the first stop. Goldenrod kept dumping fish on him until the apprentices were forced to produce a third basket to hold them all.

That was more than his fair share. The look of disbelief on Chisel's face made her want to rub it in. It was more fish than the apprentices could eat. Chisel would have to give some away before they spoiled—and explain where they came from.

They went to the common pavilion next. Goldenrod granted the guards two fish each. She kept the two biggest to feed House Applesmile. The rest went to the commons, feeding everyone who wasn't gathering their own food.

If the weir keeps bringing in that much fish we'll have some to store some for winter, Goldenrod thought.

***

"Lady Burnout? We found one of the wormy ones."

She followed the hunter outside the wall to where the infected deer was being butchered. The intestines had been dumped in a metal basin.

A glance at the bloody guts was enough to show multiple parasites were alive in there. They quivered. The sight nauseated her. Embarrassing. She'd thought nothing could bother her that much anymore.

Poking through the mess with forceps let her catch two worms, quickly transferred to a clear plastic box. The rest were too nimble for her.

"Bring me another basin. I need to take away their hiding spots."

She pulled out a two foot length of intestine and squeezed it empty with her gloved hands. Nothing. She tossed the empty sausage casing into the new basin and chose another.

The fourth one had a worm in it. That she squeezed into the small box, along with some blood. The worms turned to feasting on the deer blood.

Some of the parasites were smart enough to hide under the tubes instead of inside them. They'd have to wait until last.

"Oh, ewww!" squealed one of the hunters.

Lady Burnout turned to her sample box. Two of the parasites were eating the third, one biting just behind the head, the other working on the tail.

"Interesting. Obligate sibliphagy," she said.

"What?"

"They eat each other until only one is left. That's why Belladonna only had one in her. It was the survivor."

"Ewww," said the hunter again.

"There's stuff just as nasty on our planet." Lady Burnout tossed another worm into the small plastic arena. "Do you find any partially eaten deer carcasses?"

"Yeah. Well, how partial? There are ones with enough bits on the bones you can tell they're freshly dead."

"Any with just the belly eaten out?" asked Burnout.

"That part's always gone. It's softest. But there's always more than that eaten."

"Of course. The surviving offspring feeds on the host for as long as it can."

The hunter looked puzzled. "Didn't Belladonna's . . . parasite run off right away?"

"Yes, because there were strange creatures acting in a threatening manner. Which means these things are born smart enough to make threat assessments as well as fast enough to escape."

"That's scary."

***

Butchering a deer was a straightforward process for the hunters. They'd had enough practice to efficiently separate out the edible portions. The definition of edible was stretched to the limit to provide all the food they could.

Lady Burnout's current project was less elegant. Her subject lay on a board between two tree stumps, shaded by the edge of the forest. Instead of extracting the parasites from the latest "wormy" deer she was trying to follow the trail of damage they'd left in the intestines. Figuring out their behavior should let her devise new treatments for Strongarm. So far, she'd just wound up wondering why the poor son of a bitch wasn't dead of peritonitis.

"My lady, we found something that might interest you."

Burnout looked up from the carcass she was dissecting. Leadsmith had a tense look on his face. She followed him to the butchering station.

"This one doesn't have a worm, it's some big critter inside it. I hit it by sheer luck."

The deer carcass was suspended by the neck. Leadsmith pivoted it to face the interesting part toward Lady Burnout. An arrow stood in the beast's belly. A handspan away something poked out of a tear in the hide.

"That's certainly a parasite," she said. "Thank you."

Before trying to extract the creature she wiggled the arrow to check for reaction. Nope, it was as dead as it looked.

"Hold on to the arrow as I cut," she told Leadsmith. "I don't want it falling out."

The watching hunters held the deer steady as Burnout opened the hide with a scalpel. This parasite was at least ten times thicker than the ones she'd found before. The maw held sharp triangular teeth. Where she wiped blood or other fluids off, the skin exposed was green.

"Damn, I wish I'd saved some gloves for later," she muttered.

Cutting open intestines was messy. She stepped back to wait for the dripping to stop. Then she resumed cutting, exposing the rest of the parasite. Two arms were folded against the torso. The lower torso tapered into a tail. The arrow was stuck in the ribcage.

Lady Burnout nudged Leadsmith aside. Some leverage on the arrow let her slide the parasite out of the deer.

"Ugly," muttered a hunter. The others agreed.

She had to agree. In full sunlight it was hideous. The small eyes sat over a mouth fixed in a dead snarl. The head reminded her of . . .

"I need to check something. Don't dispose of the carcass. I want to examine the extent of damage to it. Move it to my dissection table if you need to."

"Yes, milady," said Leadsmith.

The chirurgeon was already marching across the field of stumps between the woods and the camp. Two guards stood at the gate, hands resting on the hilts of their rapiers.

They were flanked by a pair of wooden stakes with orc heads impaled on them. Lady Burnout held her specimen up to one for comparison.

Triangular teeth, check.

The skin was different shades of green.

The orc's eyes were protected by a bony ridge. Burnout had to press her fingertips to the creature's face to find its equivalent.

The ears were in similar spots on the side of the skull.

Orcs, of course, were bipedal. Burnout palpated the parasite's tail. The hips were easy to find. The lower tail held two sets of bones in parallel.

Lady Burnout stepped back to pull her thoughts in order. The big parasite was clearly a transitional form between the little worms and whatever the thing was that burst out of Belladonna's body.

She winced at a memory of a black claw cutting from the inside. Then she checked the hands of the parasite. Pressing on the fingertips found a needle-sharp point on each one.

Which made Belladonna's thing a transitional form to . . . Burnout looked at the severed head. No. She needed more data before leaping to that conclusion.

The guards were watching Burnout as a distraction from the boredom of their long shift. When she snapped her gaze to them they braced to attention.

"I have a message for Count Dirk. I need orc bodies to dissect. At least four."

"Yes, my lady!" blurted a guard. He ran through the gate.

***

"Hey, Newman, catch," said Deadeye.

Newman was almost at his tent, but he stopped and reached for the object the other hunter tossed across the lane. It was a good catch, but the feel of it against his skin shocked him into knocking it up in the air.

"What the hell? Where did you find ice?"

He caught the irregular chunk again and slid it from hand to hand. His palms grew wet as the ice melted from his body heat.

Deadeye laughed. "Plane is handing them out."

"Where the hell is he finding ice?" The cold made Newman remember life on Earth, and everything else there: showers, plentiful food, safe houses. He shivered from the flash of homesickness, not the cold.

"He's making it, dude. Plane's the newest wizard."

"Huh. How'd that happen?" Newman tossed the ice back to Deadeye while it was still big enough to throw.

"He burned himself. Was warming some venison when it fell off his dagger into the fire. Burned his fingers getting it back. Poured some water on the burn and it became ice." Deadeye's grin had a sardonic twist.

"Nice trick. Pity he didn't come up with something useful for killing orcs." Newman wiped the cold water off on his shirt and locked away the thoughts of civilization.

***

"Milady? We have the bodies you wanted."

Lady Burnout brought two baskets of gear to examine the orc corpses. She made the young fighter carry the heavier one.

The dead orcs still lay on the travois they'd been dragged here on.

Burnout chose the one on the left. She placed a chisel above the eyebrows and gave it a firm whack with her mallet. It went in just enough to crack the bone. She moved it over two inches and struck again.

Continuing the crack around the back of the skull required a break to sever the neck. Fortunately her subject had bled out while being dragged through the woods so that wasn't nearly as messy as she'd feared. When the chisel marks connected around to the forehead she used a tent stake to pry up the top of the skull. It popped right off.

Opening the torso had no surprises. After looking over the organs she began taking slices and examining them under her microscope.

The testicles were the only organ she sampled on all four bodies.

A gate guard brought Autocrat Sharpquill at her command. He kept his annoyance at the interruption down to a "this better be important" frown.

"Thank you for coming, my lord," said Lady Burnout. "I've made some interesting finds."

She led the Autocrat to the right-hand corpse. She pointed at its crotch. "This is a penis."

"You know, I was going to guess that."

She pointed at the next one. "This is an ovipositor."

"An ovi-what?"

"It lays eggs. The gametes I found in it were twenty times the size of the sperm the other one produced. They're mobile, they have a tail to push with, but they're definitely eggs."

"You're saying this one is female?" Sharpquill was no longer amused.

"Yes."

"It looks identical to the male."

Burnout shrugged. "Sexual dimorphism isn't mandatory. It doesn't even apply to all primates."

"I'm trying to figure out what this means."

"It's obvious. What they did to Belladonna, and to, to the deer, it's not a dominance display. It's their life cycle. Catch something about their own size, inject the gametes into the prey, then let it go. The gametes merge, the fetuses fight to be the sole survivor, then it eats its way out of the host. Then I guess the baby orc looks for a band to join."

Sharpquill vomited.

"That's—that's horrible," he said. "What a monstrous world we've been exiled to."

"There are wasps back home that breed that way. They're predators in both feeding and reproduction."

"They don't do it to us." He spat to clear his mouth.

Examples from her tropical disease rotation leapt to mind, but she didn't want to distract him.

"Let me show you the brain." She called over a guard to bring the severed head. "See, it's about the size of a human brain and has complex convolutions like ours. I'd say they're roughly equivalent to our intelligence."

"Just what we need. Wait—there was a report. A patrol said they saw an orc who looked pregnant. It ran off at the start of the fight."

Burnout thought a moment. "They probably have some sort of dominance hierarchy. The orc on the bottom—well. It has to be bad to be the orc on the bottom."

***

Goldenrod reached through the flap of the smoking tent. Prying a strip of fish off the line by feel was annoying, but it beat getting a blast of smoke in the face. She bit an end off the strip and chewed it.

"Can I try one?" asked Pinecone from across the clearing. It was his turn to tend the charcoal mound.

She underhanded the strip to him.

Pinecone popped it in his mouth. "That tastes good," he mumbled around it.

"Yeah. It's too moist to last. I need to dry it completely."

"Like jerky? Yuck."

"Jerky lasts. We don't know how long winter is here. We might need tons of stored food to make it through."

Pinecone stomped on the mound. A section settled in, sending a puff of smoke out the top. "Are we even going to have a winter?"

"The trees look temperate, not tropical," she said. "So probably. But until we've been here a year—or can ask some natives—we have to prepare for the worst."

He laughed. "That's it. We need to take orcs prisoner and interrogate them. 'Recite your calendar! What's today's date? Confess!'"

Goldenrod added more damp wood to her fire. "They're stone age. Probably not good at astronomy."

"There were stone age humans who were good at it. That's it! We need to quest for Orchenge."

***

"Come in, Strongarm," said Lady Burnout. She waved him to a chair instead of the examining table.

He sat cautiously. "New treatment?"

"No. New research. I've figured out what the orcs were doing when they attacked you. It's not dominance behavior. It's reproductive."

She explained the lifecycle. Gametes meeting inside the host, embryos growing into cannibalistic worms, then an immature orc. Belatedly she realized this would have been a good time to use that med school workshop on how to tell patients they have terminal cancer. The only part she remembered now was, 'Put a box of tissues where the patient can reach it'.

The whole camp had been sneezing into rags or leaves for months now.

"Well . . . fuck," said Strongarm. "I kept hoping this would be like a tapeworm or something. Y'know, something I could live with."

"I'm sorry, it's worse than that."

"Shit."

She didn't have anything better to say.

He took a deep breath. Forced a smile on his face. "We can keep doing the treatments, right?"

"Absolutely. I mean to beat those motherfuckers." She gave him a matching smile.

"Good. Thank you. Well, thanks for the news. I have to get back to work." Strongarm popped up and darted out of the tent.

***

Dinner was almost ready when they heard the herald's cry.

"All subjects are invited to Court to hear His Majesty's proclamation!"

Master Sweetbread and Mistress Tightseam exchanged glances. Neither had heard of a new law in the works. He said, "One of you go listen. Let the rest of us know what it's about."

"We'll go," said Goldenrod. She led Newman down the lane.

About a quarter of the camp was gathered before the Court Pavilion. The three thrones were filled. The full set of ladies in waiting and courtiers stood about.

King Estoc stood, reading chalked notes off a slate. "Be it known to all. The creatures known as orcs cannot co-exist with us. They perceive humans like deer: solely as food or hosts for their young."

That caused a stir among those who hadn't heard Lady Burnout's discovery. The king didn't pause.

"We call upon all Our subjects to kill orcs at every opportunity. None shall be spared because of their age or condition. Wounded must be finished off. Those fleeing must be caught and killed when practical."

Sounds of shock.

"All authorized fighters are commanded to search out and kill orcs as their other duties permit. Those wishing to join them see Count Dirk for training."

King Estoc resumed his throne. A herald announced that court was over. Some attendees bolted to spread the news. Others clustered in buzzing knots.

Goldenrod and Newman walked back in silence.

Master Sweetbread greeted them with, "What's the news?"

"Genocide," answered Newman.

***

Strongarm hastily slapped the tent flap closed behind him as he came in, clearly hoping no one saw him entering the chiurgeon's tent.

"Thanks for coming," said Lady Burnout. She waved him to the examining table.

He lay down on his back. "Where's Elderberry?"

"She's out doing some rumor control."

Burnout gathered together the gear for the treatment.

"What kind of rumors?"

"Some people noticed you and her are disappearing from sight at the same time. The two of you having an affair would explain why you're not paying attention to Foxglove any more. Elderberry is going to be visible while you're missing and hopefully divert the gossips to something else."

"What? That's crazy."

"Uh-huh. Turn over."

Strongarm's face twisted up. "Do we have to do it this way?"

"You really don't want to take this mixture orally."

He complied without grace, shoving his pants down to his knees. His hands gripped the edges of the cushioned table.

She took out a crock of venison grease but didn't apply it. "Okay. Relax. Deep breaths. Peaceful thoughts. Waves on the beach."

The first time she'd asked him to visualize a peaceful forest, which had been counterproductive.

As his muscles unclenched Burnout applied the grease. "Keep relaxing. This will be tedious but it should help."

Strongarm calmed enough to let her insert the tube. When the fluid flowed in she draped a couple of blankets over him. The stuff wasn't cold, but putting room temperature liquid in his body core was enough to produce shivers.

"Why are people telling rumors about me?" asked Strongarm. "I haven't been doing anything."

Lady Burnout was happy to divert his mind.

"That's just it. You're not doing anything. Dropped Foxglove. Not chasing anyone else. That's so unusual for you people are trying to figure out what you're really up to."

"I didn't drop her," he said defensively.

"That's what she's calling it. You two were intense for a while. Now, nothing. Or so I hear."

"Eh." He shifted on the table, not enough to dislodge the tube. "How much are you putting in me?"

"Almost done. Keep relaxing."

"I don't want to avoid her . . . but if we were hugging and she felt a parasite wiggling under my skin? I couldn't deal with her reaction."

"You could tell her."

There weren't any hints of Strongarm's infection on the grapevine. Burnout was surprised no one had figured it out. Or maybe the ones who'd figured it out were creating all those other rumors for additional security.

"I can't. God. No, there's no way I could say it. She'd be so disgusted. Or worried about the thing bursting out of my skin at her."

Lady Burnout thought he was more worried about that than anyone else could be. He'd confessed nightmares about the parasites tearing their way out of him the way they had Belladonna.

She'd given up trying to reassure him. They hadn't had even half the time needed to fully develop. He had two months left. Though the damage from the parasites feeding on him might be unsurvivable before that.

She said only, "If you gave her a chance you might get a pleasant surprise."

The man shook his head. After a pause he asked, "So who else are rumors connecting me with?"

"Me." Oops. She shouldn't have let amusement show in her voice.

"Oh. Sorry."

"Don't worry about it. It's a small price for patient confidentiality." She pulled out the tube. "That's all. Now we let it soak in a bit."

Burnout busied herself cleaning the tube and bowl.

"It's doing something," said Strongarm. "They're thrashing around more than usual."

"That's a good sign." Burnout checked the timer on her phone, blessing Sparrow for his electrical gifts.

"Or it's making it worse."

"We'll see. This is a trial and error process."

The timer let out a soft beep. Burnout pushed the metal basin closer to the table. "Okay, time to get down."

She guided him as he slid off the table. He didn't need help with the motion. She just wanted him aimed right as he squatted over the basin.

The usual scent flooded the tent, mixed with a citrus note from the acidic fruits she'd mashed into the mixture. Strongarm reached for the basket of leaves to clean up.

She said, "I see some swimmers. It worked."

Strongarm rubbed his belly. "I don't think it got them all."

"No. it's going to take a few times." She thought a moment. "More acidic might be better. I'll talk to the brewers to see if they can get me vinegar."

***

Newman tramped toward the Court pavilion. "Anybody know what this is about?"

Beargut shrugged. "The herald said the Autocrat wanted to talk to all the hunters and fighters."

The crowd in front of the pavilion looked to be everyone in those two categories plus some guards who'd never been out patrolling for orcs.

The thrones were empty. It was just Autocrat Sharpquill and a few of his slate-wielding aides.

"Take a load off," said the Autocrat as he walked into the crowd. The men obediently sat on the grass. "You've been doing great work. We're getting enough food to get by. The orcs are being pushed back. We're winning the fights with them."

Newman whispered, "Where's the 'but'?" to Beargut.

"Now we need to do something more. Take the initiative. Find a way to hit them where they're weak."

Master Sharpquill paused to let a buzz of startled remarks die down.

"I want volunteers for an expedition going South down the river. Follow it until it reaches the sea or you've been gone a week. That's the best place to find a civilization. If you find an orc base we'll mount an attack to burn it out. Who wants to go?"

Many enthusiastic shouts.

"Good. Continue with your plan for the day. Volunteers meet here tomorrow morning to start organizing. That is all."

***

"I want to go!" declared Pinecone.

Newman hadn't shared the news to recruit anyone from House Applesmile. He'd wanted to get Goldenrod's opinion before he decided whether to join the expedition.

"Isn't it dangerous?" blurted Shellbutton.

Everyone looked at Newman.

"The danger is the same as here. Plus anything new we might encounter out there. What gets you is not having a fallback when something goes wrong. Break a leg in camp, you're taken care of. Break it three days away and the rest of the team has to carry you. Two guys with broken legs . . . well, that gets ugly."

"Are you going?" asked Master Sweetbread.

"I haven't decided yet."

Goldenrod chuckled.

"I haven't."

"I know," she said. "It's so sweet that you'd consider being best woodsman in the camp, and best at noticing ambushes, and best sniper, and say, 'Maybe they don't need me. I'll just hang out.'"

That caused a few more chuckles. But not from Newman.

"I wanted to get your opinion first," he said to her. By his glance around the table he'd rather be saying this in private. "And get your permission."

Goldenrod needed a moment to respond to that. Theirs was an informal relationship. He didn't need her permission for anything. If he was asking it . . . that meant he was taking her seriously as a partner. Not just being polite.

"You have my permission," she said. "On one condition. Come back intact."

"Agreed."

They squeezed each other's hands, not sure when they'd reached out to each other. The rest of House Applesmile hid smirks.

"Do I have your permission?" Pinecone asked Shellbutton.

"Don't ask me," she said. "Ask Newman."

Gazes turned back to him.

"What's the farthest you've ever walked in a straight line?" asked Newman.

"I cover miles every day gathering wood for the burns."

"That's not a straight line. Ever walk so far you couldn't get home that day?"

"No," said Pinecone. "I wasn't a Boy Scout."

"I was. Probably everybody in the expedition will be. If you haven't done that kind of hiking you're not ready for this mission."

***

Autocrat Sharpquill had a team in mind. They'd all shown up in the crowd of volunteers. He called out half a dozen names and dismissed the rest.

Newman and Bodkin were the only hunters. Or maybe Borzhoi was counted as a hunter. The other three all wore red belts indicating they were squires, apprenticed to some knight to learn the arts of armored sword fighting and chivalric behavior.

"Gentlemen, Lord Sharpedge will be the leader of the expedition," said the Autocrat. "I'll leave you to it."

Sharpedge introduced himself as Duke Stonefist's squire. The other two were Falchion, squired to Sir Flint, and Joyeuse, who was one of King Ironhelm's squires. Sharpedge's first action was to inspect the gear and supplies everyone brought. Newman thought that was a good start.

The guy still had a butterbar reek about him.

"The plan is simple," Sharpedge said. "We're going downriver until we reach the sea, use two thirds of our supplies, or see something we need to report. We'll stay on the bluff at the edge so we have a view across the flood plain. We'll forage as we go to stretch out supplies.

"At some point we'll run into the mountain range we've glimpsed from hilltops. It runs perpendicular to the course of the river."

"Which makes no sense," interjected Falchion.

Sharpedge grinned. "Falchion is a grad student in cartography in mundane life. Crossing the mountains will be the hard part of the trip. We've requisitioned most of the available rope. Master Forge supplied some spikes and a hammer but they're not optimized for rock. On the way out I want to see how high we can get to maximize our view.

"On the move we'll have a hunter as first and last. You're best at spotting trouble. If we find orcs or anything fall back behind the fighters. Everybody ready to go?"

Newman looked over the rest of the group as they all gave a yes. The squires had pared their armor down to breastplates. He and Bodkin had similar armor made of rhino hide. Borzhoi wore a leather vest with metal plates riveted to it. Orcs aimed for the torso with their spears.

The backpacks were mundane camping gear except for Bodkin, who had his gear in a wicker basket lined with canvas that hooked onto his shoulders. Borzhoi and Bodkin had nearly as many arrows as Newman. The squires didn't have bows. They carried steel swords in easily accessible scabbards.

This was probably as good as they could do with what was available.

"Newman?" asked Sharpedge.

"Yes, I'm ready," he answered.

"Then lead off."

Newman walked briskly toward the gate. Goldenrod stood to the side of it against the inside of the wall. She blew him a kiss.

He gave her a smile and wave as he went through the gate.

***

Strongarm looked at the deposit he'd made on the forest floor. Nothing wiggled. He'd shit out orc worms after earlier treatments. The last five had done nothing. He suspected the worms had learned to escape the intestines when poison was coming through.

When he was done he went back to gathering deadfalls. The pile was spread out like a mattress. When it was two feet tall he added dead leaves.

He'd thrown up three times in the process. Burnout claimed her last potion didn't have any drain cleaner in it, but the taste said otherwise. She said surgery was too dangerous, but it couldn't be worse than dealing with more vile gunk.

Strongarm lay down on the pile. He was so tired it actually felt comfortable, once he'd twisted a branch to keep it from poking his back.

He pressed his palm against his belly button. A bit of wiggling faded as the parasites moved away from the intrusion. An aggressive one pushed back.

Strongarm held a poniard in his right hand. With the left he poked at the parasite, drawing it into pushing up his skin. The blade struck. Blood gushed out. The worm twitched and went still.

"There, I got one of you, dammit."

The wound started to hurt.

A worm's head popped out of the hole. It snapped its sharp teeth at the sky repeatedly.

"Are you laughing at me?" He swung the blade to cut the head off, but it vanished back into his belly.

"Fine. I'll get you all." He pulled the can of lighter fluid out of his knapsack and sprayed it all about him. Soaked his clothes, soaked his hair, soaked the wood on every side.

When the can was empty he took the nearly empty Bic lighter from the bag. His hand trembled. Weak from parasite damage? Or the bleeding belly? Maybe even afraid to die.

Not that it mattered.

The third spin of the flint wheel ignited the shirt cuff. Flames spread quickly from there.

It hurt more than he'd imagined. But not for very long.

***

Lady Cinnamon chalked notes on her slate as she surveyed the woodcutters. They'd cleared a swath around the camp. The open ground was dotted with stumps and carpeted with leaves and twigs stripped from cut trees.

She kept clear of the tree being cut. Two men pulled back and forth on the long crosscut saw Master Forge made. Four more stood around with axes, ready to lop off branches when it fell or swap in if one of the saw men cried uncle.

There should be another crew working but young men would rather tramp through the woods looking for orcs than cut wood. They didn't have to deal with householders demanding more wood for cookfires or Lord Goldpen diverting some for a Court campfire.

"Timber!"

A puff of dust struck Cinnamon as the tree crashed to the ground. The saw men moved along the trunk cutting the branches sticking straight up. Axemen followed behind cutting the ones on the sides.

There was a scream, muffled by the forest. The woodcutters lowered their tools and looked around.

Another scream. Then a young woman raced out from under the trees. She stopped bent over, hands on her knees, catching her breath. A "Help" emerged between pants.

The axemen were in a line facing the woods. The saw men left their tool and scrambled for the spears they'd left by the water jugs.

"Where are they?" called Leaf the foreman.

"They who?" panted the woman.

"Orcs!"

"Didn't—" pant "—see any."

"Then what's the fuss about?" demanded Leaf.

Cinnamon walked up to the woman and put a hand on her shoulder. "Relax. Just catch your breath."

She recognized the woman from the food rationing work Cinnamon did for the Autocrat. This was Ivy, a moderately productive gatherer. A member of House Chevron. Her plain brown shift was kilted up above her dirty knees.

When Ivy's breathing slowed Cinnamon asked, "What happened?"

"I found—I found . . . oh, God, it's so horrible."

"Can you take us there?"

Ivy nodded.

The woodcutters surrounded the two women as they went through the forest. Ivy went off course a few times and had to cast about to find the trail she'd been on.

There was no mistaking it when they arrived. A human body, burnt black, lying in a pile of ashes. The limbs were contorted, head thrown back in a silent scream. The hair and clothes had burned away. The shoes were only burnt at the tops. Maybe that would be enough for identification.

Cinnamon laughed silently at herself. They didn't need to identify the body, just see who didn't show up for dinner.

"Make a stretcher," she ordered Leaf.

"Shouldn't somebody else do that?" he protested. "We have work to do."

"So does everybody else. You're here. You'll take him to the grave yard. Someone else will dig the grave."

Leaf sighed and waved his men to work. They began cutting saplings and branches. An argument broke out over whether to use the partially burned branches by the body.

"Hell, no. They're dirty."

"So? The corpse won't care."

"Burnt wood is weak."

"The ones left were too green to burn. Good thing. Imagine if this had spread?"

Cinnamon shuddered at the last comment. A forest fire would ruin their chances of survival.

On the far side of the burnt corpse Ivy picked up her basket. Her collection had spilled when she panicked. Cinnamon helped her gather the plants up again, automatically inventorying them. A dozen of the fig-like fruits. Some of the leafy vine that cured scurvy. And a disappointingly small vineroot.

When the stretcher was done they had a new problem. All the woodcutters balked at picking up the body with their bare hands. Cinnamon admitted she didn't want to touch it either. Leaf solved it by cutting more wood to lever the corpse over.

As it turned a scorched metal can fell onto the ashes.

"Hey, that proves it's suicide," said a woodcutter.

"Nah, could have been left in the fire to destroy evidence."

"Who'd go to this much work to commit a murder? There's easier ways."

"I know what I'm sure of," quipped another. "I'm having fish for dinner tonight."

As the body twisted and cracked the smell of burnt meat overwhelmed the wood smoke.

Leaf cursed the wiseacre into silence.

The six men lifted the stretcher and marched toward the camp. They weren't in step but they walked slowly enough to have the proper funeral procession feel.

Cinnamon walked behind. "Ivy, go ahead and ask Lady Burnout to meet us," she ordered.

The woman scampered off, relieved to be away from the corpse. She was fast enough—or the woodcutters were slow enough—that Burnout met them at the camp gate.

The chiurgeon looked at the grisly remains without flinching. "Strongarm. Poor bastard."

"You recognize him?" burst out Leaf.

"I recognize the shoes. The size is right. And . . . he was at risk."

She and Ivy unfolded a sheet. Cinnamon noticed multiple faded bloodstains and concluded it came from the examining table. She helped them drape the sheet over Strongarm's remains.

Sighs of relief came from some of the woodcutters.

Burnout turned to Cinnamon. "Do we have Court tonight?"

"Nothing's scheduled, no."

"Then schedule it. I need to make an announcement."

***

Sharpedge wiped orange blood off his sword with some leaves. "If these things ever figure out how blades work we're going to be in trouble."

"That's why we don't let any escape," said Borzoi. He kicked a body to make sure it was dead.

The four orcs had gone down quickly. They'd thought Newman was alone and chased him into the solid formation of squires. The one that tried to get away had three arrows in its back.

The "cuk—cuk—cuk" of the local waterfowl interrupted them as a flock took off from the river. Newman had an arrow nocked as they came overhead. He hit one in the breast. It landed fifteen feet from the expedition. A second arrow also hit its mark. That bird landed the same distance away on the other side.

"I guess we're having lunch early," said Sharpedge.

***

The bluff veered east away from the river as they approached the mountains. A lake formed where the river met the ridge. The land had been gradually descending the whole trip. It looked to keep descending until it reached the mountains, much to Falchion's disgust.

Orcs were scarce. They hadn't seen any since the handful they'd killed on the second day. The Autocrat's hope that they'd find the spawn point of the orcs was looking slim.

When they reached the base of the ridgeline Sharpedge directed them back toward the river. The going was rough, though they weren't forced to break out the ropes. Falchion pointed out sharp corners and rough surfaces on the peaks as signs of recent uplift. Erosion hadn't smoothed anything yet.

As they drew closer to the river a roar became audible. The sound of a waterfall. They couldn't see the drop but from the noise it must be spectacular.

"Oh!" said Falchion. "I'm an idiot. These mountains aren't uplifted at all. They're a crater rim."

Joyeuse looked back and forth along the ridgeline. "Craters are round."

"Anything round looks straight when you just have a small piece of it."

The six men contemplated this a moment.

"That's a hell of a big crater," said Newman.

"Let's keep going," said Sharpedge.

Climbing to the top of a foothill let them see the river as it passed through a gap in the ridge.

Falchion had to shout to be heard over the waterfall. "That's not erosion. There must have been a gap in the crater wall when it formed."

"No, something knocked a hole in it," Newman shouted back. "See those horizontal marks on the far side of the gap? That looks like a wall I saw after a shaped charge blew it open."

"Okay, that would do it. But the blast would need enough energy to throw the debris downrange where it wouldn't dam the river. You'd need a nuclear weapon for that much energy."

"Or magic," said Joyeuse.

They watched the river roar through the gap for a moment.

Sharpedge broke the spell. "Let's go back and find a pass we can get through. There's no game on bare rock. We're eating and drinking what we carry now. Let's hurry."

The two passes closest to the river were impossible. Sheer cliffs blocked the way, impassible without spikes and ropes. Sharpedge didn't want to chance that without proof whatever was past them was easier to climb.

The third was passable. Barely. Joyeuse claimed to have rock climbing experience. "And I don't mean those pansy gym walls." He went up the slope barefoot until he found a spot to secure the rope.

The rest followed up, one on the rope at a time. Newman carried the squire's boots, tied to his backpack.

That brought them to a quarter mile of walkable, if rough, rock before the next steep point.

Joyeuse took off his boots again. At the top he cried, "Thalassa!"

"What?" said Sharpedge.

Borzhoi explained, "He sees the ocean."

Once they'd followed up they could all see the ocean. The ridge sloped down gently in some spots, was a cliff over foaming waves in others. To the right they saw the river pouring into the sea, higher than Niagara Falls.

"Anyone see a ship?" demanded Sharpedge.

"I don't see a damn thing," muttered Bodkin.

"There's something flying over there." Borzhoi pointed left along the ridge.

The others said no. Newman rooted in his pack. He emerged with Lord Orrery's binoculars.

"Where's that flyer?" he asked. He followed Borzhoi's arm. "Dragon."

Sharpedge cursed.

Newman began a slow scan of the horizon.

Falchion said, "I think those islands formed with the crater. Looks like molten rock splashed into the sea and solidified."

"Islands don't do any good," complained Sharpedge. "They don't even have anything growing on them."

Borzhoi pointed at the closest. "That one looks like one of Longshanks' Welsh border castles."

Sharpedge closed his mouth. Newman thought he might have counted to ten. "Okay, can anyone think of a reason to go down to the ocean?" asked the leader. "There's clearly no towns or ships."

"I'm curious if that's a saltwater or freshwater sea," said Falchion. "But that can be another trip."

"Fine. Let's head back. If we make good time we won't have to sleep on rock tonight."

***

"Lady Burnout! Lady Burnout!"

An experienced physician can tell from tone of voice whether a call for help indicates hypochondria, attention-seeking, or a real emergency. This one was exhausted, frantic, and scared, the worst combination.

Burnout grabbed her bag and burst out of her tent. The messenger was bent over, hands on knees. The moment he saw her he straightened and trotted back the way he came.

She followed. A description of the emergency would be nice, but if the boy didn't have the breath for it she wouldn't bother haranguing him.

It was obvious when they reached the main gate. A mixed group of hunters and fighters were hauling wounded men on stretchers and travois. The gate guards were taking stretchers and putting them down against the inside of the wall. Another fight with the damn orcs.

People from the camp were already coming forward to help with the casualties. The wounded were moved into well-spaced rows and first aid begun. More stood about, willing to help but unsure how.

"Find someone bleeding," she directed. "Put your hand on the wound and push hard enough to make the bleeding stop."

They scattered among the bodies.

One casualty had been laid off by himself with a tunic over his face. Lady Burnout went to check on the field diagnosis. Lifting the cloth revealed the point of a spear broken off in the man's throat. He couldn't have lasted more than a minute or two. She laid it back down.

Blood was oozing through the fingers of the nearest volunteer. She strode over to her. "Push harder."

"I am pushing."

"This hard." Burnout put the palm of her hand over the other woman's and leaned into it.

The volunteer gritted her teeth but didn't complain. She shifted her weight.

When Burnout lifted her hand off no new blood appeared.

"Good, keep it like that." She moved down the line, applying more pressure whenever she saw the need. Every time she released her hand the bleeding had stopped.

When all the bleeding was controlled she started disinfecting. Bites first. She'd already fought a nasty infection from an orc bite. She was careful not to waste the disinfectant. It was distilled from the remaining liquor in camp. The distiller wept over some of the whiskey he ruined.

After the bites were the punctures. Then it was time for real triage. No belly wounds this time, thank goodness. Even the hunters were wearing rhino-hide breastplates. Now if only the rapier fighters would put some heavier gear on instead of "relying on mobility."

The bite wounds came first again. Stitching them closed took careful maneuvering to find intact skin close to the ragged tears. Spear wounds were quicker. A stitch or two, if any, and a firm bandage to keep it closed.

"Excuse me," said Lady Burnout, waving aside the man standing over the next patient.

"I'll be back when she's done with you," said King Estoc.

The fighter tightened his jaw as she worked on his arm. When Burnout picked up her bag he asked, "Will I keep it?"

"Yes, probably. Keep an eye on it for redness or tenderness. Let it heal before you start using it again or you'll cause extra damage."

"Yes, my lady."

She hoped it wouldn't develop an infection. She'd brought a wide variety of antibiotics but most were gone now.

***

Sharpedge reported failure but Autocrat Sharpquill was full of praise for them.

"You've discovered more about the local area than we have in all the time since we arrived. You proved we can do deep reconnaissance safely. And you've also demonstrated cooperation between factions which haven't always done so. You will have Their—His Majesty's thanks in Court."

"I don't know if we can do this safely in other directions," said Sharpedge. "We didn't see orcs on the way back until we were within a couple days of camp."

"Not a worry for today. Gentlemen, thank you. Please rest for two days and then resume your normal duties. We'll do another of these in a few weeks."

***

Goldenrod punched Newman in the chest. "You're late," she said.

"We took the scenic route." He pulled her into a kiss. There were no words for a few minutes. Fortunately, they had the Applesmile pavilion to themselves.

She broke off the clinch.

"Right. Do I need a bath?" Newman still grinned.

"No. Well, yes. But—I guess the Autocrat didn't tell you the news."

"What news?"

Goldenrod took a deep breath. "Strongarm is dead."

"What? How? I thought he was staying in camp."

"He was. He . . ." Another breath. "He killed himself."

The chairs were all outside. Newman sat down on the rug. "I knew he'd been beaten hard enough to be left for dead, and it broke him, but he seemed stable. Why?"

"It was worse than that." Goldenrod relayed the announcement Burnout made of rape, parasitic infection, and unsuccessful treatments.

"Damn. Just . . . damn." Newman stared at the wall, face tense. "Did they have the funeral already?"

"Day before yesterday. Lord Pulpit did well by him. I can take you to his grave."

"Yeah. I'd like to pay my respects."

The graveyard was on the downstream side of the camp. They took the path down the bluff slowly, not wanting to catch up to the four young men carrying a blue plastic tank from one of the portapotties. The path was much improved. Stones and split logs provided traction through the slippery spots. In some places it was even wide enough for them to walk side by side.

Strongarm's grave was bare dirt. The others were all covered in weeds. The oldest graves had some growths a couple of feet tall. Their wilted flowers had kept them from being cut down by visiting friends.

Only Strongarm had a visitor now. Foxglove knelt by the grave. Tears cut lines through the dirt on her face.

"Again?" muttered Goldenrod, barely loud enough for Newman to hear her.

Newman studied the markers on the other graves. Round pieces of wood two or three feet tall were carved with names and decorations. Some had Celtic knotwork, others animals or weapons. Berry juice stained the wood to highlight the work.

There was no marker on the new grave. Well, that kind of work took time.

Goldenrod addressed Foxglove in a gentle tone. "How are you holding up?"

"Eh."

Newman sat cross-legged at the foot of the grave. If he'd been alone he would have spoken aloud. Instead he hoped somewhere Strongarm could hear his thoughts.

Thank you, Strongarm, for welcoming the new guy. Thank you for sharing your joys and opportunities with me. Thank you for not being angry when I beat you at something. I'm sorry I couldn't be what you needed me to be to let me help you with . . . that.

His gut twinged as he imagined the parasites Strongarm suffered from. *I don't know how long I could have stood it.*

Then he sat and stared at the grave.

Foxglove broke the silence. "I was so *angry* at him. We *had* something. He was still immature, but we were building something together. Then he got hurt and . . . it stopped. Lots of 'I'm still too sore.' And then avoiding me. And . . . and I didn't push because I have my pride."

She ripped a handful of grass up and threw it at the grave. "Damn it, why couldn't he tell me?"

Goldenrod put a hand on Foxglove's shoulder. "He was probably afraid you'd freak out."

"Well, yeah, it was freaky shit. But I'd get past it. I could've helped him. At least held his hand."

Newman said, "Men don't like admitting weakness. I ran around for hours with a sore ankle because it was my first patrol and I didn't want the guys thinking I was the kind of doofus who'd sprain an ankle in combat. Then we got back in the track and blood came out of the top of my boot and I realized I'd caught some shrapnel."

Goldenrod was giving him a strange look. Maybe he shouldn't've told that story.

After a minute to digest that Foxglove demanded, "If guys get to be so private about stuff why is Burnout spreading his business around? She told everybody everything."

"Because suicide is contagious." Newman's voice was firmer this time. "If people think he just gave up because it sucks here it's that much easier for the next guy to decide, 'hell with it, I'm checking out.' And we can't spare anyone. Now—no matter how bad it sucks he's not being eaten alive by worms. And the next one the orcs rape knows to start treatment right away."

***

Autocrat Sharpquill assigned workers to haul fish from the weir and spear slow-learning cuttlefish. Ostensibly to save Goldenrod from the manual labor, it let him control distribution. She'd retained the right to take a few fish each day.

Today she'd brought Redinkle along to help carry. They were commiserating about Foxglove's latest breakdown as they walked back to the bluff.

"Isn't that your garden?" asked Redinkle.

"Hmmm? Oh, the vineroot planting. Yeah."

"I thought you'd been spending more time on it."

"Not since I started the weir. Root vegetables don't take much work. Let's see how they're growing."

They ambled over to the patch she'd hoed out of the flood plain.

Vines had sprouted from the chunks of vineroot Goldenrod had planted four months before. Most were twice as long as when she last checked on them. The rest were failing, the leaves wrinkled and brown at the edges.

"Oh, crap." Goldenrod nudged one of the dying vines with her toe.

A furry head poked out of the ground. She jerked her foot back as yellow teeth snapped at her. The sudden motion made her fish start thrashing again. It broke her grip, falling into the weeds. The critter squeaked an imperative and ducked back into its hole.

Two similar heads popped up with squeaks of their own.

Goldenrod let out a stream of curses. She picked the fish up by its tail.

"Looks like they've eaten about a third of the patch," said Redinkle.

"Right. Time to hunt some rats." Goldenrod gripped her fish firmly as she marched toward the bluff.

At the tent she picked up her hoe and a militia spear. Mistress Tightseam joined the pest control expedition with another spear.

Goldenrod was not in the mood for conversation on the walk back to her garden plot. Tightseam didn't try to start one.

The critters were too nimble for Goldenrod to spear them. After working off some frustration with stabbing attempts she switched to the hoe. Caving in the burrows under the garden forced the critters to go above ground to another hole. Tightseam held her spear ready to impale them when Goldenrod flushed them out.

Once two had been speared (and finished off with the hoe) the third critter fled into the weeds of the flood plain.

Goldenrod hoed through the dead portion of the vegetable patch without flushing any more. When she paused to wipe the sweat from her face Tightseam said, "The good news is you have it ready for replanting."

"Yeah." Goldenrod's breathing broke up the words. "Have to go—find some wild ones. To chop up for eyes."

Tightseam held out her hand for the hoe. Goldenrod handed it over. The older woman moved into the remainder of the patch. The hoe blade gently pulled vines aside before chopping at the base of the tall weeds.

"Did you bring your spinning wheel?" asked Tightseam.

"No."

"What about your inkle loom?"

"Where would I have put it?" Goldenrod let some exasperation leak into her voice.

"Calligraphy set?"

"I brought an embroidery project. A favor with my device for Newman to wear at the archery tourney," snapped Goldenrod. "And I haven't worked on it because we're trying to survive. What's your point?"

Mistress Tightseam chopped under another weed, pulling it out with most of its roots. "My point is you keep starting things and dropping them when something else captures your attention. That's fine for a crafter in the Kingdom. Try everything, find your love.

"But we're trying to survive here. You can't drop something unless someone else is going to pick it up. Showing people how to find food in the wild, that's great. Dozens of women are out looking for vineroot. The weir's too big to keep to yourself.

"Now this—" Tightseam waved at the garden patch. "This is yours. You claimed it. Nobody else is going to mess with it. So you need to follow through."

Goldenrod kicked at one of the dead vines. "I am following up."

"No. You need to check on it every couple of days. Chase off that critter before he comes back with friends. Take out weeds before they get this tall." Tightseam hoed down one standing above her knee.

"Hmph."

"You're a dilettante. That's fine back home. The Kingdom attracts dilettantes. Some pass through, some stay until they've sampled everything. Some settle down. We can't afford that here."

She stepped closer to the younger woman. "We especially can't afford someone as talented as you wasting her efforts."

Goldenrod flushed. "Most of it is luck. I didn't know how many fish were out there for the weir to catch."

"Fine. We can't afford your luck being wasted."

***

Lady Burnout looked up from her notebook as a patient came in. He limped into the chirurgeon's tent, supported by a cane on one side and his wife on the other.

"How's the foot, Lord Barrel?" she asked.

"No better," he grunted.

"All right, up on the table and I'll take a look."

"Do I have to?"

Burnout gave him a stern look—but he'd had a hard time climbing up on the previous visit. "Fine."

Elderberry turned the big chair around for him then set a footstool before it. Burnout dragged up another footstool to sit on.

Barrel sat and put out his right foot. His wife slipped the shoe off of it.

"Thanks, Dandelion," said Burnout. She unwound the brown-crusted bandages.

The puncture wound on the sole of the foot still dripped pus. The red swelling reached around to the top of the foot. Yes, not any better.

"Well, that antibiotic pill didn't help any," she said.

"Time for a full course?" asked Barrel.

"I don't have enough left for a full course. And if it's ignoring a single dose ten might still not be effective."

"Plus you'd want to save them for someone more useful than me."

Burnout nodded.

Dandelion bristled then subsided as her husband put a hand on her arm. "Don't be mad, sugar. It's her job to make those decisions. What can you do for me?"

"I think it's time to amputate."

Barrel laughed. "My GP always told me I'd wind up losing a foot if I didn't keep up with my meds. Guess she's finally right."

Burnout was grim. "You might not survive the amputation. And it might not get all of the infection."

"How long have I got without it?"

"Three days. Maybe five."

Dandelion gasped and clutched her husband's hand.

"Then let's cut."

***

"You want us to do what?" demanded Master Chisel.

"I can cut the flesh," explained Lady Burnout. "But going through the bone will take strength. It has to be done *fast*."

The carpenter looked over his apprentices. "We don't do fast. We want it done right. Hmmm. Plane, think you can do this?"

The burly apprentice flinched, then straightened. "Aye."

"Go sharpen the saw then."

Lady Burnout took charge of the rest of them. The apprentices carried the examining table and most of the other furniture out. A plastic tarp covered the rugs. A chunk of log used as a stool came in to act as the cutting surface.

Barrel and Dandelion exchanged a few kisses. Then Burnout sent her back to their own tent to await the outcome.

In the corner Elderberry sharpened knives and scalpels. She'd changed into her worst dress, already stained from helping with less drastic procedures. She reminded Burnout to go change.

When everything was ready Barrel lay down on his back, right foot resting on the log.

"Want a shot of whiskey?" asked Elderberry.

Barrel laughed. "Don't bother. One shot won't do a thing to me. If you have a bottle that'd keep me from feeling pain."

"Sorry. Only have a couple of shots left."

"That does it. If I live through this, to hell with the Autocrat, I'm going to find out what kind of beer you can make from vineroot."

"I'll drink it," said Master Chisel.

Elderberry drew tight the tourniquet just below the knee. She twisted the metal bar until Barrel let out a grunt of pain, then locked it down.

Noses wrinkled as Burnout popped open a Tupperware container.

"What is that, concentrated piss?" snarled Master Chisel.

Burnout didn't answer him as she swabbed the leg. Boiled urine was the best disinfectant she had left.

"Right. Hold him down," ordered Lady Burnout.

The carpenters, along with a couple of royal guards who'd been standing around idle when Burnout looked for help, grabbed Barrel's limbs and shoulders.

"Forgot one thing," said Chisel. His knife cut a fist-wide chunk from the end of his belt. He held it before Barrel's face.

"God, we are being old-fashioned," said the patient. He bit down on the leather scrap.

Lady Burnout looked at the lines she'd drawn on the shin and calf. Still looked right. She picked up the biggest knife.

The blade went in smoothly. She followed the leg as it bucked, snapping, "Hold it still!" at the guard bracing the ankle.

The sounds she ignored.

Elderberry continued the cut on the other side. Blood covered the log.

As Elderberry finished her cut of the calf Burnout switched to a scalpel for finer work, going by feel to reach the bone.

Then she switched to the top, carving loose a flap of skin to meet the angled lower cut.

Elderberry took hold of the edge and held it up as Burnout worked along the bone.

"That's it, shift." Burnout sat back. Elderberry moved to straddle Barrel's legs, both hands holding up the flap of flesh.

Plane took her spot, saw at the ready. "Where do I cut? It's all covered in blood."

Lady Burnout's left hand wiped blood off the bone. Her right guided the saw to just below the swelling of the tuberosity.

Jaw set, Plane started cutting.

Burnout wondered if the screams were louder now, or if she was just noticing them with no work to distract her.

The leg jerked free of the guard's sweaty grip, knocking the saw away. Burnout lunged to get hold of it. She and the guard held it still again.

Plane cursed as he realized he'd started cutting a new notch in the bone. A little fumbling put the saw back in the original cut. Plane pumped the saw faster.

A cracking sound was followed by Plane declaring, "Done!"

"Still need the fibula," said Burnout. She picked up her scalpel and cut between the bones.

"Right. Sorry. Forgot."

"Now. Right there." Burnout held the broken ends of the tibia apart as Plane slipped the saw between them to reach the other bone. The side of the saw blade felt cold on her thumb. *Now I understand how those old time surgeons took an assistant's hand off.*

The second bone didn't take nearly as long. A few strokes with the scalpel severed the last tendons connecting the lower leg to the knee.

"Get that out of my way," snapped Burnout at the guard holding the severed foot.

More disinfectant went on the open surfaces. Then Elderberry pressed the upper and lower cuts together. Burnout started stitching the edges together.

The screams stopped.

"Is he okay?" asked an apprentice.

"Crap, he's seizing." Elderberry yanked the leather out of Barrel's mouth. Her hand went to his neck. "No pulse."

She began chest compressions. Ribs cracked under the strain.

Lady Burnout added three more quick stitches then started mouth to mouth.

After a few minutes, Elderberry gasped, "Switch." Burnout took over compressions.

An apprentice said, "Milady, I'm CPR qualified."

"Take it."

A second came forward to relieve Elderberry.

A third one stood ready to relieve the man on the chest. When they prepared to switch Lady Burnout said, "Wait. Check him."

Elderberry reported, "No respiration. No pulse."

"Then I'm calling it."

Shoulders slumped all around the circle.

Burnout used the log to push herself upright. "My lords. Thank you for your extraordinary efforts. You will be thanked at Court. That we couldn't save him is no reflection on you. I'll have someone else come take him to the graveyard."

"You're welcome, my lady," said Master Chisel solemnly. He looked at his blood-splattered crew. "Let's go get cleaned up."

Elderberry said, "I'll get a stretcher crew. And . . . I'll tell Dandelion."

"Thank you."

Lady Burnout sat on the tarp to hold vigil over the man she'd failed.

***

Screams woke Newman up. Everyone else in House Applesmile was waking up. The screams were coming from outside the tent. Lots of them.

He pulled his boots on, grabbed bow and quiver, and pushed through the tent flap. People were running about in a panic. The screams were growing louder. Newman picked out shouted battle cries amid them.

The heart of the commotion was toward the gate. Some people were heading that way. All armed.

The other members of House Applesmile had come out and were demanding explanations. Newman stepped up on a haybale. A couple of the pavilions near the gate had collapsed. That shouldn't be causing this much panic.

Someone ran down the lane shouting, "To arms! To arms!"

That would be more useful if Newman knew what to use his arms on.

The Wolfheads were armoring up. Whatever it was they were taking it seriously.

Newman nocked an arrow. He wanted to be ready if there was a threat out there.

Shellbutton screeched, almost startling him off the haybale. "Orc orc orc!"

She was pointing toward the fence.

Newman turned. An orc was climbing over the top of it, one leg swung over and feeling around for a toehold.

He loosed the arrow into its back. It penetrated the spine just below the ribs. The orc dropped and lay still.

Shouts in the Wolfhead encampment indicated more orcs had come over their part of the fence.

"Everyone grab a knife," said Master Sweetbread.

More orcs popped up over the fence. Newman put one arrow in an eye, another in a throat. A third orc kept climbing with an arrow in his chest. An arrow in his belly made him fall on the outside.

He missed his rifle. It was better for a stream of pop-up targets than a bow. But at least here they weren't shooting back at him. As the orcs came up faster he drew and loosed in a steady rhythm.

Wolfhead Alpha called, "First squad hold the fort. Second and third squads with me." Armor jingled as they double-timed toward the gate.

Newman pulled the last arrow from his quiver. How many had been in there? He'd lost count. It flew into an orc's open mouth, knocking him off the fence.

Newman felt a tug at his belt. He glanced down to see Goldenrod dropping a handful of arrows into his quiver. "Thank you," he said.

They smiled at each other for an instant.

When he looked back at the fence two orcs had landed on their feet. They stalked forward, spears level.

An arrow in the heart put one down. The other kept coming with one in its chest and another in its belly.

Newman put a third arrow into it, penetrating the other lung. It kept coming, running now.

"Why won't you die?" snapped Goldenrod.

The orc fell onto its face, landing a few feet from her.

Three more landed on the grass inside the fence. They bent to pick up the spears they'd dropped while climbing.

Newman waited for the left hand one to straighten up and put an arrow into its throat.

"Die, you," said Goldenrod. The middle orc fell.

Newman shifted his aim to the right hand one.

Goldenrod said, "Die."

The orc collapsed.

There weren't any live orcs in sight.

"Did you do that?" asked Newman.

"I, I think so," she answered. "I felt something when I said that to the first one. Now I'm doing it on purpose."

Two green heads popped over the fence.

"Die, die."

They vanished.

"Did you get them?"

"Yes. I can feel their deaths."

Behind them Pinecone muttered, "She's killing them with magic."

Goldenrod leaned against Newman's leg. "Ooh. I feel lightheaded."

He slung his bow over his shoulders, hopped off the haybale, and scooped her up in his arms. "Right. You just focus on orcs. I've got you."

Redinkle stepped up beside them. Red flames flickered on her fingertips. When the next orc appeared she flung the fire toward it. The flames dissipated inches from her hand. "Dammit!"

"Die," muttered Goldenrod.

"Keep practicing," said Newman to Redinkle. "You might have a good hand to hand attack."

He looked at the rest of House Applesmile holding cooking knives. "You don't want to let orcs get that close. Grab tent poles. Use them as clubs."

No more orcs were appearing on their stretch of fence. Shouts and clangs said the Wolfheads had visitors.

"Let's go help." Newman carried Goldenrod into the Wolfhead encampment. One tent had collapsed, another was halfway gone. Orcs and fighters and their ladies were all mixed in a chaotic brawl.

Goldenrod didn't need to aim, just choose. "Die die die. Die die. Die. Die."

The single orc left went down under a flurry of sword blows.

"What the fuck?" demanded Borzhoi. He stabbed a fallen orc.

"Magic, man," said Newman. "Shit."

Goldenrod had fainted. Her head lolled against his chest.

"We'll take care of her," said Mistress Tightseam. She and Shellbutton took Goldenrod from his arms. "You boys best go fight."

Sweetbread, Pinecone, and Pernach stood behind her, ready to follow Newman's lead. The cooking knives were tucked into their belts. Each held a seven foot oak pole with a blunt steel spike at the top.

"Right. Fight's over here. Sounds like it's going badly there. Borzhoi, you coming with us?"

"No. Our orders are to stay here."

Newman wanted to push it but he had no authority over Borzhoi inside the camp.

"We'll keep an eye on your place," said Borzhoi.

"Right." Newman readied his bow. "Let's go."

His three housemates followed behind him single file.

Newman stopped to put them in a formation. "Make a line, side by side. Close enough you can hit an orc in front of the guy next to you. Keep the line straight."

He spotted a crafter watching them, uncertain whether to advance or flee. "Hey, you. Grab a pole and join the line."

The crafter promptly fell in next to Pernach. Two more men saw this and joined the line. They made it wide enough Newman had to walk down the lane ahead of them instead of beside.

The melee at the gate made the mess at the Wolfheads look like a ballet. Orcs were everywhere. All the pavilions lay flat, furniture pushing up through the canvas to trip distracted fighters. The

Wolfheads were in a circle, surrounded by orcs trying to find a gap in their armor.

"Move left," ordered Newman. "End man touch the wall." He pointed to show where he wanted them standing.

Here and there orcs stood still, catching their breath or looking for a new target. He loosed arrows into them. He didn't dare fire on the ones engaged with people.

"When I'm out of arrows we'll advance," he said.

Instead orcs came to them. Not in a line. It was a gaggle, orcs deciding individually to attack this new threat. They closed fast enough the pole swingers didn't have a chance to gang up on any of them.

Newman tossed his bow aside as two came for him. One had his last arrow sticking out of its chest. He drew his Ka-bar knife and let them close.

The one with the arrow rushed around, coming at Newman from his right. Newman hopped to the side, making it come between him and the second orc. A pivot let the spear go past him.

He braced the knife, holding it still as the spear slid over it until the orc rammed its hand into the blade. It grunted, lifted the hand off the spear, two fingers dangling loose, and stepped back.

Newman followed, pushing the spear up with his left hand. The point of the Ka-bar went under the orc's ribs. A twist as he pulled it out released a gush of orange blood.

The other orc jabbed at his head, almost too fast for Newman to duck. He felt it brush against his hair.

It was too far away for him to reach. The orc braced the spear with one hand while the other thrust it at him in quick jabs. Two hops kept him alive but he couldn't keep that up. One stumble would kill him.

On the next jab he spun forward, pressing knife and hand and chest against the side of the spear, shoving it away.

The orc swung the butt of the spear at Newman's leg. That would bruise. He continued the twist, pulling his knife through the orc's throat. Rancid blood sprayed into his face.

Newman wiped his eyes with his left hand. A glance told him his militia wouldn't hold much longer.

Poles met spears to become a shoving match. The orcs were stronger. Sweetbread, at the end of the line, was already down on one knee.

Newman rescued his host with two quick stabs to the orc's back. He lunged to the next one and stabbed it in the back of the neck before it realized its neighbor had fallen.

The orc facing Pernach heard the death grunts. It pivoted, raising its spear to knock Newman's knife arm aside with the haft.

The blow stung. He didn't drop the knife but pulled back to make sure of his grip.

The spear turned, point aimed at Newman's belly. Then it dropped as Pernach smacked his pole into the orc's shoulder.

Newman side-stepped to stay clear as Pinecone swung his like a baseball bat into the orc's face. Blood sprayed. It fell.

He ran along the back of the last three orcs. Attacked from side and rear they died quickly.

"Great work, men! Now let's get the line straight again." Newman saw one of the volunteers stagger to the fence and sit down against it. Blood squeezed through fingers pressed over a belly wound. Dealing with the casualty would have to wait.

Cheers came from men among the tents still standing.

Newman grabbed an orc spear off the ground. He flung it sideways at the nearest cheerer. "Never mind words! Grab a spear, grab a pole, join the line!"

A dozen men came forward with a mix of improvised weapons. Two men with swords came out of the melee and joined the line. Newman stood in the middle with a spear. The line now reached from the fence to the lane, facing the besieged Wolfheads.

Newman called instructions. "We'll walk slowly. Keep the line straight. When anyone's fighting stop the line. Keep it straight. Now, walk!"

When they were all moving he shouted, "Wolfheads, we are coming!"

Some of the orcs attacking the Wolfheads ran when they realized they'd be hit from behind. Others were too angry or too focused. They died, and the heavy fighters facing them unfolded their circle to outflank the rest.

Orcs in threes or sixes came out of the scrum, looked at the line, and went back in search of easier prey. One stepped out and flung a spear at them. A man went down with a groan.

The orc picked up another spear and hefted it. Newman flung his at it. He missed. The orc looked at the other spearmen changing their grips and went back into the melee.

Someone handed Newman two more spears.

The Wolfheads gave a cheer as the last orc facing them died.

Alpha stepped out of the pack facing Newman. "That won't let us have a continuous line," he said, waving at the pile of debris that had been the Royal Pavilion. Even collapsed it was taller than a man.

"Agreed. I'll take my men around to the left."

Wolfhead Alpha held his sword vertically in front of his face in salute.

Newman waved a spear in reply. He turned back to his men. "Start walking! You men at the tent, come stand behind us. Take the place of anyone who falls."

The melee gave way before Newman's line. Orcs went down under the poles or were distracted enough for one of the humans in the fight to stab them.

An orc lunged at the poleman beside Newman. The man flinched back, leaving a gap in the line. The orc grinned, looking for a new target.

Newman met the orc's gaze. They thrust at each other simultaneously. Newman pivoted, deflecting the orc's spear with his own and sliding it to push the point toward the orc's belly.

That didn't work on this one. It leaned in, pushing Newman's spear flat against his chest. The human dug in his feet and pushed back, trying to keep from being forced out of the line.

The orc had more weight and strength. This was a contest Newman would lose.

Then a sword cut into the orc's neck, splashing more orange blood onto Newman. The orc fell, revealing a man wearing a knight's belt. He bled from scalp and chest. One arm hung limp. He staggered through the gap in the line and collapsed.

The flincher stood a few feet away, still holding his tent pole.

Newman snarled, "Get back in line, you. And stay in line." He looked left and right. "Straighten the line!" he shouted. "Stay right between the man on your left and right."

Some men stepped onto orc bodies as they obeyed. The ground under the brawl was covered with bodies. Mostly orc. Enough humans lay among them to scare Newman. Even if they won this fight, had they lost too many to survive?

Orcs were backing into the line now as the melee squeezed them out. Poles and spears took them down quickly when they came in range.

Newman saw the Wolfheads advancing on the other side. They were putting the pressure on. In some places fighters were so close together they couldn't swing a weapon. Some dropped swords and spears to strangle each other.

Knights and squires were coming through the line. The wounded or exhausted would walk a few paces for safety then lie down. The fit waved polemen into the second line and took their places.

"Hold the line steady, boys," called Newman. "We're the anvil. The orcs are being hammered on us."

He could see a few orcs going back out the gate. Usually wounded. One was missing an arm. But a steady trickle were hale orcs who seemed to have had enough.

In humans this would start a stampede. Once a few left the rest would flee to make sure they weren't the last one left fighting. He'd seen a local unit do that in the Sandbox. In three minutes it went from ninety percent strength to a panicked mob.

Orcs didn't notice some of their number departing. Or didn't care. Their morale didn't break.

As the two lines came closer together the number of orcs still fighting dwindled. They didn't group up to defend themselves. The last dozen standing were surrounded and went down almost simultaneously.

Fighters who'd been in the melee leaned on their rescuers, panting. The lines broke up to see which humans among the bodies could benefit from first aid. Those without medical skills made sure all the orcs were dead.

Newman joined a solemn circle of men. They surrounded a dead body. Two spears had been driven crossways through his torso into the ground, holding him almost upright on his knees. It was King Estoc. A circle of orc bodies had fallen facing him, two and sometimes three deep. His sword, soaked in orange, lay on one knee.

He backed away, letting those who knew the king better mourn. He waved at his troops to spread out. All the wounded men were being helped now. If they were fit enough to walk, or be carried, they were taken away from the slaughter.

As Newman walked he stabbed the orcs he stepped over, in case they weren't quite dead. One twitched hard enough he put a half dozen holes in it to make sure.

Near the gate he found Duke Stonefist.

The duke was surrounded by dead orcs. Headless orcs, armless orcs, orcs cleaved to the spine. Stonefist lay atop the pile, unmarked. His heart had given out with the labor. His expression was frustration that he'd been interrupted in the middle of his work. The axe was gripped firmly. Blade, haft, and hands were covered in orange blood.

Newman knelt and closed the duke's eyes.

***

Constable sat on the roof of the wrecked Royal Pavilion, leaning against a box holding some of the fabric off the ground. He lifted one hand to wave to Lady Burnout. Blood leaked through the fingers of his other hand until he added the first's pressure to his thigh again.

"Fool old man," she scolded. "You need to leave brawling to the young ones." Burnout knelt to look at the wound.

"This mace isn't for show. All of us were needed."

"Right. Well, I have some news for you. Found a new magic user," she said.

Constable hissed as she swabbed antiseptic into the spear wound. "Who?"

"Me." Lady Burnout laid her hand over the flowing blood, barely firm enough for him to feel it. When she lifted it the wound was scabbed over.

"Useful," grunted Constable. The pain was still there.

"Works from the inside out. I think I can treat internal bleeding too."

"Keep your hand off my chest."

"I'll only use it for good. When you're on your feet I need you to look into some others."

"More new magic users?"

"Maybe. Just rumors. A woman claims she escaped orcs by hovering out of reach. Another guy was flinging stuff around with his mind. And the rumors about Lady Goldenrod are—well. I shouldn't prejudice you."

Constable lifted his leg, gritting his teeth as he flexed the torn muscles. "If they're real I'm calling it proof of my magic-under-stress theory."

"I won't argue."

The man used his mace to turn onto his bad knee. Burnout balanced him as the good leg pushed him upright. "Right," he said. "This thing is too damn short. Hand me a spear, will you?"

She pried one out of the hand of a dead orc. Constable held it as a walking stick. "That's good. Back to work, you."

Lady Burnout nodded. She turned and walked three paces to the next casualty.

Constable leaned on the spear as he surveyed the battlefield. It was a lumpy green carpet of orc bodies. Well over a hundred of them. The ground was soaked with orange blood turning brown as it dried.

Hardly any human bodies lay among them, though red splotches showed where some had been carried off. Lady Burnout wasn't the only one tending to the wounded. They were too busy to be questioned.

He decided he needed a drink to replace the blood he'd lost. And wherever he did that would be a good place to hear rumors. He hobbled away from the carnage.

***

Constable and Lady Burnout timed their visit to House Applesmile for after dinner that night. They arrived just as Pinecone and Shellbutton finished drying the dishes.

"Good evening. We'd like a word with Lady Goldenrod," said Constable.

"That's fine," said Mistress Tightseam. "We were going to take a shift at the hospital tonight." She and her husband excused themselves.

Pernach said he needed to check on the charcoal burn. Redinkle offered to help light fires. Pinecone and Shellbutton followed without providing excuses.

Goldenrod waved to the seats across from her. "Please, join us."

Newman sat beside her like a stone, silent and not moving without the application of force.

"This isn't anything formal," said Lady Burnout. "We're just chatting with those who've displayed magical abilities. Hopefully we can learn something about how they work."

"So this is about me offing those orcs."

Constable said, "We're very glad you could stop them," in a reassuring tone.

"What have you heard?"

"Many rumors, mostly contradictory," said the retired cop. "We'd like to hear your own description of what happened."

"We were right here. Orcs were coming over the wall. Newman was shooting at them. One had three arrows in it and kept coming. I was scared and angry so I yelled at it. It fell down."

"Do you remember your exact words?" asked Constable.

"Yes, but I'm avoiding saying that word."

"That's a perfectly reasonable precaution. Would it be safe to spell it?"

Goldenrod hesitated. "I guess so. I said, 'Why won't you D-I-E.' It fell down. And . . . I didn't just know it had from the falling down, I could *feel*, somehow, that it was D-E-A-D."

Lady Burnout said, "There's others feeling stuff like that. Sparrow can sense if a battery is charged. I can detect bleeding, even internally."

"Redinkle says she can feel where fires are in the charcoal mounds," added Goldenrod.

"What happened after the first one?" asked Constable.

"Newman was shooting more. They were coming faster than he could shoot. So I said it again. Said it shorter. Just saying the one word worked. I tried just thinking it but nothing happened."

"There's rumors you passed out."

"Not at first. Each time I did it—it didn't take an effort to say it, but the first few times I felt one D-I-E it was like I'd picked up something too heavy to carry. Tiring."

She put her hand on her boyfriend's arm. "Newman had to carry me to the Wolfhead encampment so we could help with that fight. Then it was harder, like each time I said it I was punched in the stomach."

Newman sat up in alarm.

"Not too painful. I kept myself awake until it was over. Then—I can't really say if I passed out or just fell asleep."

"Looked like passing out to me," said Newman.

"When I woke up the battle was over," Goldenrod finished. "I'm still sore." She stroked from sternum to bellybutton to show where the pain was.

Constable asked, "Have you tried to use this power on a human or animal?"

"No!"

"Have you said anything else that happened to come true?"

Goldenrod thought a moment. "When we arrived Mistress Seamchecker took us out to look for edible plants. Someone thought it was hopeless so I gave her a pep talk. Right after that I found the first vineroot."

"There's another time," said Lady Burnout. "When you brought Redinkle in with her hands burned you told her she'd be fine. I didn't want to argue in front of the patient but I figured she'd get back to fifty percent use of her hands at best. Instead she doesn't even seem to have scars. Your magic is the best explanation I can think of."

"Wow," said Goldenrod. "I didn't realize I could do that. It's—wow."

"I hesitate to ask you to help directly. We could easily get into a monkey's paw situation. But if there's a critical situation, would you . . .?

"Of course. But I think I shouldn't use this for anything non-critical."

"I disagree," said Constable. "Abilities need practice to develop strength and control. You need to exercise this talent so you know the costs and limitations."

"You mean I should follow through with it?"

"Exactly."

"I will."

Lady Burnout stood. "Thank you for being willing to discuss this. Please let us know if you discover anything interesting."

"Certainly."

The investigators strolled off.

It was Goldenrod's first private moment with Newman since the battle. "Does it bother you that I can do . . . that?"

He smiled. "I always thought you were magical."

She poked him in the ribs. "Seriously."

"I am being serious. You can say something and an orc dies. I worked with guys who'd talk into a radio and blow up a building. Or a town. Yours is magic. Well—we're here."

Goldenrod shivered.

"Want a hug?" he asked.

"Yes." She leaned into his arms.

"Come on. I could use a cuddle too."

Newman led her into the pavilion. Their zipped-together sleeping bags were in a corner, open to air out. A moment sufficed to shed shoes and outer layers.

He laid down on his back. Goldenrod lay over him, head on his chest. His arms went around her, firm, not squeezing. They breathed together for a while.

"I had a horrible thought," said Goldenrod.

"Oh?"

"When we realized what Belladonna did to us we chased her into the woods."

"I remember."

"Later we found out she'd been caught by some orcs and raped. That left her with a parasite that ate her alive from the inside."

When she didn't continue Newman said, "Yes."

"I said 'I hope the worst thing ever happens to you.'"

Goldenrod's calm tone now didn't match his memory of the words. They'd been filled with rage. She'd hurled them like a weapon after Belladonna.

"I think I got my wish."

She went silent.

Newman thought about it. "It makes sense. I'm not saying you made it happen, just that the theory makes sense."

"To think that I did that to someone. That's horrible."

"Belladonna is responsible for everyone who was killed since we arrived here. Even if all the wounded pull through that's over twenty people."

"She deserved to be punished. But I'm not a court. And even if we decided to execute her—eaten alive?" Goldenrod shuddered.

"If a little kid gets hold of a pistol, I mean a kid who's never been taught safety, doesn't even know what a trigger is. If that kid kills someone with the pistol, it's not the kid's fault. It's the fault of whoever let him get hold of it."

He could feel the tension in Goldenrod's body. She was listening, but hadn't relaxed. She wasn't accepting the analogy. Or hadn't made the connection.

"When Belladonna brought us here she gave a pistol to everyone with any aptitude for magic. You didn't mean to shoot her. It was an accident. In a sense she shot herself."

Now she relaxed.

Newman held her. When Goldenrod began to snore he smiled.

***

Newman let the tent flap fall shut behind him as he said, "Good morning, my Lord Autocrat."

He walked a few paces forward, restraining his hands from locking to his sides. This wasn't his company commander. His body still ached from the strain of yesterday's battle but he'd be damned if he'd show it with all those with real injuries about.

"Thank you for coming, Newman. Please, sit. Are you thirsty?" Autocrat Sharpquill wasn't in his embroidered court robe, just a plain tunic for working in.

"No, thank you, I'm fine."

Declining refreshments didn't hurry up whatever this was. The Autocrat sat looking at Newman for as long as it would have taken to find cups and pour tea.

Newman waited him out.

"You're a hero, you know," said Sharpquill.

"I didn't do much," Newman answered with a grimace.

"Perhaps others did more. They didn't get your results."

That didn't demand an answer.

"People want to acknowledge what you did yesterday."

"I'm not much for ribbons and such." There were a few in a box that had only been opened to put the last one in. A box still on Earth, and not missed.

"The Kingdom prefers titles, headpieces, or just bringing people up to be cheered by the whole populace. There's some as suggested a lordship for you as the traditional first award but that wouldn't satisfy the crowd."

"So, what, you want to knight me?" asked Newman.

Sharpquill laughed. "I won't say you haven't earned it. But you're not qualified to fight in armor. That's the definition of a knight here. If the title went to someone without that qualification—well, I wouldn't want to deal with the reaction."

"So what do you have in mind?"

"To make you a baron. You get a fancy hat and are called Your Excellency, but there's no meetings to go to."

Newman contemplated this a moment. "Baron. All the barons and baronesses I've met were couples."

"We can certainly elevate you and Lady Goldenrod together. She's accomplished much." The Autocrat seemed happy to make a concession.

When Newman didn't ask for more Master Sharpquill continued, "Given the loss of King Estoc and Queen Camellia, the elevation will be on the authority of King Ironhelm and Queen Dahlia."

He said this with a bit of tension, as if Newman would consider this bad news.

That made a few pieces of camp gossip fall into place. "You don't want to have a tournament to pick a new crown. Just have the visiting monarchs move over to reigning."

"Yes. We're too close to the edge to take time out for a tournament. That duel was bad enough."

"So when I accept the title from them I'm accepting their legitimacy. And committing my prestige to them."

"Yes."

That called for a moment of contemplation. "Okay. I've only heard good things about them. We can use all the stability we can get."

Autocrat Sharpquill let out a long breath. "Thank you. That settles one side of it."

"I thought we were done." At least, he'd hoped.

"Oh, we've made good progress on my political problems. Found a present for your girlfriend too. But that's all favors you're doing for other people. Not anything you want."

"I don't want anything," said Newman.

"See, that's your superego talking. Or conscience. I like the Freudian terms. Superego, ego, id. You have a muscular superego. Everything you do is for duty or honor. You don't ask for rewards. You just accept what rewards come to you in due course."

Newman's face was still.

"But your id. Your id is a fucking accountant. It measures everything you've done. Kept a lot of us from starving. Turned that battle. No, don't wave it off. I was there. You were at least the feather at the pivot. Now your id is counting all that up. And counting what you're receiving. And it's going to get unhappy if they don't balance. People with unhappy ids do stupid shit. So, Newman Greenhorn, deep down, what reward are you hoping for? Never mind if it's actually possible. That's my problem. What do you want?"

The silence stretched out. The Autocrat looked patient. Newman's gaze wandered the tent, touching on the hanging tapestries, chalked-on slates leaning against tent poles, and sheaves of papers. A closed laptop lay on the table.

"Goldenrod and I, we'd been keeping it calm. Both wanting to move slow. This was going to be our first full weekend together. After all we've been through I can't imagine my life without her. I want to marry her."

Sharpquill nodded.

"But . . . I don't want to say, 'hey, let's get hitched,' and leave her thinking I just proposed because we're stuck here and all the other girls in camp are taken. I want to propose dramatically so she knows I mean it. But I can't buy a ring here and there's no safe place for a romantic proposal."

Newman felt his heart pounding. He took slow breaths to calm himself.

Master Sharpquill was trying to suppress a smirk. "For a place, why not during Court? Pageantry and plenty of witnesses."

"I can't interrupt the Court!"

"Who said interrupt? We'll put it on the agenda."

"Then it ruins the surprise."

"The only people who need to know it's on the agenda are Their Majesties and the herald. They've kept bigger secrets than that."

Newman grinned.

"It's settled then. A fancy ring, and we let you say a few words after you and Goldenrod are elevated."

"How are you going to find a ring that fits her?"

"I'm not. I'm going to delegate."

***

"How did it go?" asked Mistress Tightseam as they returned to House Applesmile that afternoon.

Goldenrod sat down hard and said nothing.

Newman took the seat next to her. "I found one of those squirrel-like things. She tried but it didn't work."

"Dammit, I said D-I-E a dozen times and the thing just sat on a branch and laughed at me."

Mistress Tightseam said, "Good. Now you know something you didn't before. That's what experiments are for. Finding out what happens."

"That wasn't very useful to find out," muttered Goldenrod.

"Sure it is. You're learning one of your limits. That's important."

Redinkle gave Goldenrod a mug of water. She drained it and handed it back.

"A limit is when I know it won't work. Sometimes it works and sometimes it doesn't is just random," said Goldenrod.

"I'm glad to know it's not automatic," said Newman. "I was wondering if I'm actually good at hunting or if it was just all the times she said 'good luck' when I left."

That earned him a fist in the ribs. He grinned at her.

Tightseam focused on analyzing the magic. "It worked on the orcs, not on the squirrel. We need to find the possible differences and find experiments to test them. Different locations. Different moods. Whether the target is a threat. Does it only work at home?"

"No. I found the vineroot by the river."

"Right. So what do the orcs, healing Redinkle, and finding vineroot have in common that the squirrel doesn't?"

"The orcs and Redinkle's burn were both scary," said Newman.

"But the food search wasn't," countered Tightseam.

Goldenrod looked up. "No, I was scared. I was putting up a good front but landing here, facing starvation, wondering if someone would steal our food—I was scared all day."

"Then that's a new hypothesis—your powers work when you're scared. How can we test that?"

"I'm thinking." Goldenrod stood up from the table.

Newman said, "Heights are an easy fear to trigger. We could set up a rappelling line. It feels scary but it's perfectly safe."

The campfire burned briskly, providing warmth and light on this cool evening. The cooking rack had been put away after dinner, letting it burn unobstructed.

Goldenrod didn't answer Newman. She stared at the fire, concentrating on the problem. Redinkle hadn't been scared when she first started a fire. She was frustrated and angry. Goldenrod focused on the fatigue and tension from the unsuccessful experiment. Added jealousy of Redinkle controlling her powers so easily. Imagined people mocking her for not being able to be useful. Her pulse beat in her ears as her blood pressure climbed. The fire was ignoring her, mocking her magic. She ground her teeth. She wanted to stomp on something. Stomp out the fire, but it was too big.

Goldenrod said, "This fire is out!" as she shoved her hand into the flames.

The fire vanished. Blackened wood sat in a pile. The last wisps of smoke drifted away, no more following them.

Goldenrod fell back, hands clutched to her chest. "Ow ow ow ow."

Newman's chair fell over as he rushed to her. "Let me see your hand," he said, prying it open.

The hand was unharmed.

"Ow. Not hand. Ow. Chest hurts. Ow. Ow. This fire is lit."

The flames flared up to their previous strength. Newman grabbed Goldenrod and rolled them away from the fire.

"Okay, that's better." Goldenrod disentangled herself from her boyfriend and sat up.

"What the hell was that?" demanded Newman, still prone.

"An experiment," said Mistress Tightseam. "Executed without any of the planning or review for safety we'd discussed previously."

"It worked," said Goldenrod.

"Then why did you fall down?"

"The spell worked. But it wasn't just a punch. It hurt like a sledgehammer to my chest. Relighting it eased it some."

Newman looked from her to the fire and back. "Killing an orc, that just takes a slice to a nerve or artery. A small change. Putting out the whole fire all at once—that's a big change."

"Finding the vineroot didn't take any change. Just a bit of steering." Tightseam paused.

Newman realized Belladonna also just needed a little bit of steering as she ran through the woods.

"What about the healing?" she continued.

Redinkle had her hands over the fire as if she was checking for changes. "It took me a week to heal. She made changes slowly."

Goldenrod took her seat again. "Then I've learned two limits today."

***

The next day Goldenrod put magic aside to focus on gardening. Her mind was on critter traps as she walked down the lane. When another woman stepped in front of her she absent-mindedly started to go around.

"Lady Goldenrod, I need to say you haven't been thanked enough for all you've done for us."

"Oh, um. Thank you." Goldenrod recognized her as Mistress Filigree, one of the master crafters.

"Not nearly enough. May I give you a hug?"

"Uh—all right."

Goldenrod reflexively reciprocated Filigree's hug. It was firm but brief. As they parted the craftswoman took both of Goldenrod's hands in hers.

"My dinner last night was a stew of fish with diced vineroot. All I could think was that without you I'd be having a hungry night, if not starved to death already."

She emphasized this by interlacing her fingers with Goldenrod's.

The younger woman, overwhelmed by this unexpected affection, but too polite to rebuff someone whose council she wanted to join, put on a rigid smile.

"But I'm so rude, keeping you from your work. Please forgive my excess of feeling."

Once released Goldenrod muttered thanks and headed for Master Chisel's shop. Maybe one of his apprentices would have an idea for traps.

When Goldenrod passed around the corner the head crafter joined Filigree.

"Well?" asked Mistress Seamchecker.

"Left ring finger is five and a half," said Filigree. "Need any of the others?"

"No, the boy's a traditionalist. We don't have any five and a halves though."

"That, my dear, is what ring stretchers are for," said Mistress Filigree.

***

The first order of business at Court was Master Sharpquill and other senior officers swearing oaths to King Ironhelm and Queen Dahlia as the new monarchs. There was no grumbling. Everyone was in enough shock that the simple changeover was met with relief.

Then the monarchs began inducting people into the newly formed Order of the Partisan. Everyone not an authorized fighter who'd hit an orc with some kind of weapon received a hastily whittled two inch spear with an ornate point to wear.

Goldenrod wasn't included as magic was not a recognized weapon.

There was some teasing as Lady Foxglove received hers for braining an orc with a frying pan. "It was closest!"

The official fighters received traditional awards of escalating significance. At the end of the sequence four squires were knighted. Only two had their knights with them for the ceremony.

Newman expected to be next but service awards were given out to those who'd helped treat the wounded. Again, at various levels.

"Relax," whispered Goldenrod. "It's no big deal. Kneel on the pillow, say the words, get the hats, and we're done."

He nodded.

They finally finished investing Lady—now Mistress—Cinnamon into the Council of Organizers to recognize her work setting up a hospital for the battle casualties.

The herald called, "Lady Goldenrod, Newman Greenhorn. Present yourselves to Their Majesties."

They held hands as they walked up the narrow carpet. Two cushions awaited them in front of King Ironhelm and Queen Dahlia. Newman knelt before the King, Goldenrod the Queen.

King Ironhelm was not someone who needed a microphone to be heard by a crowd of hundreds. "In the Kingdom a Baron is a leader. Most Barons have a place and they lead the people in that place. But there are other forms of leadership. To recognize them we have the Barons and Baronesses of the Court. Let us recognize the leadership we have seen.

"Lady Goldenrod, you have shown us how to find the food we needed to survive in ground and water.

"Newman Greenhorn, you've led hunters, teaching them woodcraft and survival. But your greatest leadership was when you gathered those who wished to fight the invaders and did not know how. You showed them how. You led them to battle. And at the moment of greatest crisis you tipped the scales.

"It is now Our pleasure to create you Baron and Baroness."

The herald stepped forward, "Do you, Goldenrod and Newman, swear fealty to King Ironhelm and Queen Dahlia; and do you swear that you will obey Their lawful commands, that you will treat courteously with all, whatever their degree or station, until the King depart from His Throne, or death take you, or the world end?"

Together they said, "I so swear."

The monarchs together recited, "And We swear now Our fealty to you, and swear to you We will protect and defend you with all Our power, until We depart from Our Throne, or death take us, or the world end."

Hovering ladies in waiting handed coronets to the King and Queen. Queen Dahlia smoothly placed hers on Goldenrod's head. King Ironhelm reached toward Newman, flinched, and took a step closer. Newman noticed a bandage under the sleeve of the King's tunic. The coronet landed firmly.

The herald led the populace in three formal huzzahs.

The king and queen wiggled their fingers to indicate it was time to rise and return to their places.

Newman took Goldenrod's hand as they stood. As they turned he stopped her facing him.

King Ironhelm kicked a cushion between them.

Newman knelt and took Goldenrod's other hand.

Her expression was nervous and wary.

The crowd was quiet, a few "oohs" tipping the less clued in that something was about to happen.

Newman swallowed. "Lady Goldenrod. When we arrived here I didn't know you well. I knew I wanted to know you better. Now I do know you. I'm glad we're together. In this world or any other I want to spend the rest of my life with you. Will you marry me?"

He let go of her hands to extract the ring from his pocket. He held it up to her with both hands.

Goldenrod was bright pink. Her hands wrapped around Newman's. She stammered, "Y-yes. Yes. I will," barely able to force the words out.

A buzz of "what did she say?" began in the crowd.

King Ironhelm proclaimed, "She said yes!"

The populace broke into cheers. Newman slid the ring onto the correct finger. He stood and kissed her.

The cheers went on as the kiss continued.

Then they broke apart and went back down the carpet hand in hand, wearing identical foolish grins.

A duke stepped out of the crowd. "Brave man. Can you sleep well knowing she can kill you with a word?"

Newman looked him in the eye. "Can you sleep well knowing your wife can kill you with a pillow?"

With half the camp mourning dead and more tending wounds this was no time for a fancy wedding. Lord Pulpit came by to perform the ceremony. Master Sweetbread stood as best man, Redinkle as matron of honor. Then the rest of the household found things to do elsewhere to give the newlyweds some privacy.

Newman joined Goldenrod in their zipped-together sleeping bags. They kissed.

"Is this forever?" she asked.

"Yes, forever," he said.

***

The members of House Applesmile nodded respectfully as Duchess Roseblossom approached their table. They would have stood if she hadn't waved Master Sweetbread back down when he rose from his seat.

The respect wasn't just for her title as Duchess. Roseblossom was the widow of Duke Stonefist, the Lord High Executioner. King Ironhelm had declared her the inheritor of his post as judge. She'd accepted, but changed the title to Lady Justice.

While no one at the table was aware of any crimes they'd committed there was nervous wondering over the purpose of the visit.

"Lord Newman and Lady Goldenrod," said the duchess. "I wish to give you this present in honor of your wedding."

A lady in waiting came around her and knelt, holding up a long object wrapped in cloth. Duchess Roseblossom unfolded the wrappings. It was her late husband's lochaber axe.

Newman gulped, remembering when he'd last seen it, clutched in the dead duke's hands.

Now the axe was polished clean, gleaming in the rays of the setting sun. A few nicks marked the edge where a notch had been too deep to be ground out in the sharpening.

Newman stood and picked up the weapon. He hefted it lightly, then planted the butt between his feet. The haft came nearly to his chin. The crescent-shaped blade stretched from his belly button to the top of his head.

"I'm not worthy of this," he said.

"Young man, you have no idea how refreshing it is for me to hear that," said Duchess Roseblossom. "I've been hearing from knights and squires how much they deserve it since my husband's body was cold."

"I'm very sorry for your loss, Your Grace."

"He was a great man," added Goldenrod.

"Thank you." Roseblossom looked at Goldenrod. "My dear, your share of the present is the tears of all those who were hoping for this."

Goldenrod tried to suppress a smirk, failed, and said, "I think I can guess a few of the names."

"Keep guessing, there's more than a few."

Newman pivoted the lochaber axe in his hands. "I have no training in how to use this."

"Stonefist mentioned you had a good feel for it when he came back from the fence building. You actually held it as an axe, not a sword. That was the first time I heard of you. I think he'd be happy for you to have it."

He straightened. "Then I thank you for your kindness, Your Grace."

***

Ithuil was gathering herbs when the summons came. He didn't bother with the rest of the foxears patch, just shoved the cut leaves into his bag and started trotting homeward. He hoped the sorcerer would remember sending him on the task and not be angry at how long it took him to arrive.

The sorcerer was not angry.

He greeted Ithuil wearing a broad grin. "Drink! We're celebrating." He shoved a wooden cup into the apprentice's hand.

Ithuil sniffed at the cup. His nose tingled. He sipped. It was purewine, magically filtered from normal wine to concentrate the power of the drink. This *was* a celebration. He'd not tasted purewine for decades.

All five senior apprentices and the three juniors were present. This might be the most people there'd ever been in the hollow tree. A scrying pool was operating in the center. The junior apprentices knelt around the pool. All three had blood trails down their arms where they'd bled to create the pool.

The sorcerer let them share the bleeding? He was in a good mood.

Ithuil sidled up to Ymer. She'd been the lowest ranked senior apprentice before his elevation and thus happiest to see him join the group. "What are we celebrating?" he whispered.

Ymer laughed. "When we did the weekly check we found our master's pets just slew a hand of hand of hands of those vermin. You can see the bodies."

The scrying pool was focused just above the camp. There was no missing the pile of bodies. Puddles of orange blood lay between the unmoving green flesh.

"How did they get so many in one place?" Ithuil asked. "Just lure bands in and kill them in the same place?"

Ymer shook her head. "I measured the decay. They were all killed three days ago."

"Clearly the short ones led them into a trap." Osdul spoke with the arrogance of the most senior apprentice. "Look how they were confined by the wooden walls and the narrow gate. Once the killing started the green vermin couldn't escape."

The sorcerer pulled the stopper from another flask. He took a long pull, his throat bobbing as he drank. "Ah! Whose cup is empty?"

Everyone's, or close enough. Ithuil drained his cup while his master was on the other side of the room. After getting his refill he stared at the scrying pool some more.

"If it was a trap they did a sloppy job of it. I see broken shelters and dead short ones," he said. Then a chill hit him as he realized he'd challenged Osdul. Maybe he hadn't heard.

The top ranking apprentice appeared at his elbow. "The knocked down shelters were the other side of the trap. And how do you know the vermin killed the short ones? They could have been executed for cowardice."

Ithuil wasn't drunk enough to defy Osdul twice. "Of course. I hadn't thought of that."

The sorcerer was drinking from the flask again. "Oh, the vermin had the initiative. They have only two responses to a threat. Attack to claim their hunting range or flee to find an empty place. I've been scrying for bands in the region and placing suggestions that they attack. They did attack. All together. Better than I'd imagined."

He giggled and took another swig.

Ithuil thought the sorcerer must be drunk if he was blabbing so much about an experimental spell.

Or was it experimental? If he could steer the minds of vermin, could he do it to elves?

He bit his tongue as the impulse to ask the question out loud flared in him. The sorcerer would kill him for that, and possibly kill everyone who heard the question.

Insulting Osdul would just get him poisoned.

The next volume, The War Revealed, is coming soon!

About the Author

Karl Gallagher has earned engineering degrees from MIT and USC, controlled weather satellites for the Air Force, designed weather satellites for TRW, designed a rocketship for a start-up, and done systems engineering for a fighter plane. He has, on a few occasions, put on armor and been hit in the head with a stick. His sole moment of martial fame was being one-shot in Crown so efficiently there was a three paragraph write up in the kingdom newsletter. He is husband to Laura and father to Maggie, James, and dearly missed Alanna.

About Kelt Haven Press

Kelt Haven Press is releasing print, ebook, and audiobooks by Karl K. Gallagher. For updates see:

www.kelthavenpress.com

Subscribe to the newsletter for updates on new releases.

Made in the USA
Las Vegas, NV
28 December 2021

39737656R00115